美國的國際詩人會頒給沙白的詩「化粧(Cosmetics)」卓越獎

沙白（涂秀田）1995年榮獲國際詩人獎

星星愛童詩...
Stars Love Children's Poetry

著・沙　白 Sar Po
譯・陳靖奇教授 Prof Ching-chi Chen, Ph.d.
圖・張財通

錄目 Contents

黃榮村序（考試院院長／前中國醫藥大學校長） ……6

毛連塭局長序 Foreword-By Mao Lianwen ……8

苗栗縣長徐耀昌 Foreword by Yao-chang Hsu ……10

南投縣長林明溱 Mingzhen Lin ……12

澎湖縣長賴峰偉 Feng-wui Lai ……14

林良理事長序 Foreword by Lin Liang ……16

許漢章校長序 Xu Hanzhang ……22

藍芸序 Lan Yun ……26

自序 Preface ……32

民生報報導 The Happiest Day for Dr. Tu Shiu-tien ……36

月亮和星星 The Moon and the Stars ……38

太陽月亮星星 The Sun, the Moon and the Stars ……40

太陽和星星 The Sun and the Stars ……42

太陽和星星 The Sun and the Stars ……44

太陽星星燈光 The Sun, the Stars and Light Bulbs ……46

太陽 The Sun ……48

電燈 Light Bulbs ……50

黑夜 The Black Night ……52

中秋月 The Mid-Autumn Moon ……54

2

月夜 The Moon-lit Night	56
春天 Spring	58
夏天 Summer	60
秋天 Autumn	62
冬天 Winter	64
春風 Spring Breezes	66
風箏 The Kite	68
風 Wind	70
風鈴 Wind Chimes	72
春遊 Spring Outing	74
山 The Mountains	76
雲 The White Clouds	78
雨 Rain	80
海 The Sea	82
水 Water	84
湖 The Lake	86
海浪 A Sea Waves	88
湍流 Turbulence	90
河流 A River	92

- 自來水 Tap Water ……94
- 鼻子會唱歌 The Nose that Can Sing a Song ……96
- 時間 Time ……98
- 鐘 The Clock ……100
- 鐘錶 The Watch ……102
- 手指 The Fingers ……104
- 溫度計 The Barometer ……106
- 尺 The Ruler ……108
- 鞋子 Shoes ……110
- 路 The Road ……112
- 口香糖 Chewing Gum ……114
- 茶杯 A Tea Cup ……116
- 乞丐 A Beggar ……118
- 衣服 Clothing ……120
- 公寓人 Inhabitants in Apartment Houses ……122
- 馬桶 The Toilet Bowl ……124
- 汽車 The Car ……126
- 房屋 The House ……128
- 春天 Spring ……130

4

春天 Spring	132
樹木 Trees	134
老榕樹 The Old Banyan Tree	136
柳樹 The Willow Tree	138
樹下讀書 Studying under the Tree	140
竹 The Bamboo Tree	142
紅蘿蔔 Carrot	144
螢火蟲 The Firefly	146
蝴蝶 The Butterflies	148
啄木鳥 Woodpeckers	150
牛 The Ox	152
動物園 A Zoo	154
烏龜 The Tortoise	156
作者簡介 An Introduction to Tu Shiu-tien (Sar Po)	158
陳靖奇教授簡介 Translated by Prof. Ching-chi Chen, Ph.d.	164

沙白的童詩　黃榮村（考試院院長、前中國醫藥大學校長）

沙白是位專業的牙醫師，但更廣為人知的，他是一位長年勤於筆耕，熱心參與國內外核心詩會活動，在國內外都享有名望的詩人。他一生寫了不少童詩，而且還不是一般應景的，他大部分都包含有詩歌中的重要元素，如比喻、象徵、與想像力。沙白的童詩都很精簡，但它們大部分都包含有詩歌中的重要元素，如比喻、象徵、與想像力。也就是說這是給所有人看的詩歌，其中最關鍵的當然就是，孩童們聽了耳朵都會豎起來，而且一聽再聽。

他走入兒童的世界，跟著他/她們思考跟著感覺走，親近兒童喜歡的事物與具有童趣的題材，譬如說：天空、星星月亮太陽、自然界、風水山海、小動物與動物園、玩具與家具、家人、學校等等。這些題目無一不可入詩，無一不是詩。

假如沙白沒有回歸初心，只是當作詩來寫，則很快會在進出之間被敏感敏銳的小孩抓到，成年人也會很快看出是為賦童詩而強做幼稚之語而已。所以沙白的高明在此，簡單也在此，因為他很快回歸初心融入場景，唯有在此基礎上，與兒童一起呼吸一起共感，用同樣的語言，都是朋友，所以詩行走到後面，若忍不住偶有教化之語，也是自然而然冒出來，孩童也能很快入心。

我們都曾有過童年，大部分的人多以鄉愁與懷念，來回憶觸接自己的童年，我們對童年其實還是很有感覺的，只是有點像隔岸相望，中間有一段很長的心理距離。我們應該有更好的方式可以回去童年，與現在的小孩成為朋友，一起生活在大家有共同感覺，用同樣話的成長與學習環境。感謝沙白，他為我們這些寫詩的人，做了一個難得的示範。我們不見得回得去，但是至少我們知道這是可能的，因為沙白經常回去。他用豐富多元又簡短的童詩告訴我們，兒童們其實都在那裡等著我們，要我們有空就一起來玩，一起走入有共同感覺的世界。

6

A Foreword
Sar Po's Children's Poetry

— **Jong-Tsun Huang (黃榮村), former President,
the Examination Yuan, Republic of China;
former Minister of Education, Republic of China;
and former President, the Chinese Medical University at Taichung.**

Sar Po, a well-known dentist and a well-known poet, has been diligently working on the writing of poetry. He has been in good association with other poets in their daily contact and during some important gatherings. Other poets write poetry for the general reading public; yet, in addition to poetry for the general reading public, Sar Po writes children's poetry which is easy to read and is loved by children. In it, he structures his imagination through the eye of children with some rhetoric techniques, such as comparison (metaphor and simile), symbols, etc. His poetry has been enjoyed by adults and children.

In his children's poetry, he leads us, adults and children alike, in the world conceived through the eye of children. In the poetry, objects such as the sky, the sun, the moon, stars, the sea, rivers, and mountains; living things in and out of botanical and / or zoological gardens; toys and furniture; the school and the family, are all his topics.

Let us suppose if Sar Po did not go back to the primordial state of the mind intentionally and wrote his poetry, some sensitive juvenile readers would still be able to locate the existence of the mind in the poetry. The mind is the children's mind. Each and every one of us, adults and children, harbors the children's mind. Sar Po is good at grasping the children's mind in his poetry, so much so that it appeals to adults and children alike. The poetry is enlightening and educating.

Everyone has had his / her childhood and is nostalgic about it. The nostalgia is similar to that of his hometown. There is a long distance between adulthood and childhood; yet, many desire to go back to the latter. There must be a way with which one may go back to it. It seems to me that one may do so in living with children and share with them the nostalgia. I am thankful to Sar Po in giving us the possible way to go back to our childhood, not in the real world but in imagination, in his poetry. Many of his children's poems are concise and full of images conceived through the eye of children. Reading the poems would make it possible for us to be with children and lead us back to our own childhood.

台北市教育局毛連塭局長 序

童詩是兒童心靈自然流露的結晶。

童詩是啟發兒童心靈的最佳鑰匙。

童詩是教育兒童的最佳讀物。

兒童是國家未來的主人翁，教育兒童是大人的天職。大人寫的兒童詩，對兒童詩想的啟迪幫助很大，也可以豐富兒童天真純潔的心靈。

我國是文化大國，自古以來，文學興盛發達，而詩是文學的精華，歷代如金珠玉環的燦爛詩篇，一直滋養着人類的心靈。

童詩乃詩之一環，近年來蓬勃發展。沙白為詩人醫生，醫術精湛，於求學時期即熱愛文學，今於行醫之餘，仍對文學研究和創作不綴，並有傑出之創作，今將其童詩出版，為兒童詩壇綻開鮮麗的奇葩，供給大家欣賞。

前高雄市教育局長
現任台北市教育局長

民國七十五年七月

Foreword

— By Mao Lianwen, Commissioner, Bureau of Education, Taipei City and formerly Commissioner, Bureau of Education, Kaohsiung City.

Children's poetry is a crystallization of a spontaneous overflow of the children's emotions.

Children's poetry is the best key to open up the mystery of children's mind.

Children's poetry is the best text for children to read in the education of them.

Children are the future of our nation. To educate them is the duty of us the adults.

The adults write poems for children and, through them, we may enlighten their mind and enrich their innocent imagination.

Our nation is one of rich culture. Since ancient times, the production of literature has been abundant. Poetry is the essence of literature. Verses and poems, which are like gold pearls and jade bracelets brilliant to the eye, nourish the mind of the humankind.

Children's poetry has been flourishing in recent years. Sar Po, a poet and dentist, is excellent in his dentistry and in his love for literature. He was enamored of literature in his younger days. As a practicing dentist, he is still interested in doing research in and writing literature. The outcome of his writing is here for us. This collection of children's poetry is something awesome for us to enjoy.

苗栗縣政府
Miaoli County Government

涂院長秀田 惠鑒：

　　時序季夏荔月之際，蓮渚風清，梅庭月朗，敬維諸事，百務迪吉，維祝維頌！

　　素仰 院長學養卓越，奉獻醫學揚名國際，長年勤於文學創作，成就頗豐，績效斐然，深為各界仰望與敬重，文壇譽為「國際詩人」，曷勝抃賀！

　　欣悉 院長大作「星星愛童詩」、「星星亮晶晶」、「唱歌的河流」三本兒童詩集，與國立高師大前英文所所長暨文學院院長陳靖奇教授合作翻譯成英文，並編印成華英雙語的雋永詩冊，供為兒童雙語文學之優良讀物。

　　今喜見大作付梓在即，耀昌願以歡喜之情樂以為推薦，讓優良文學創作得以向下扎根，以培育更多的後輩文學人才，啟發無窮無盡的創新。

　　　　　　　　　　　苗栗縣長 徐耀昌 敬上
　　　　　　　　　　　民國 110 年 07 月 23 日

耀昌用箋

Dear Dr. Shiu-tien Tu:

At the time of mid-summer, when all kinds of fruit are ripe and flowers are blossoming, I wish you well.

Your reputation as a dentist and an international poet is well known to us. It is also known that you are well learned and have written extensively in prose and poetry.

It is a pleasure for us to find that three collections of your children's poetry, Twinkle, Twinkle, Little Stars, Stars Love Children's Poetry and Singing Rivers, will be published with their Chinese and English texts. The English rendition was done by Ching-chi Chen, Ph.d., Professor Emeritus of English, National Kaohsiung Normal University. I believe that our children will benefit from the reading of them.

Knowing that their publication would be good for education of our students / pupils, I strongly recommend them to our teachers and parents.

With best regards, I am
Sincerely yours,
Yao-chang Hsu (徐耀昌),
Magistrate, Miaoli County, Taiwan,
Republic of China.
July 23, 2021.

大家都曾上牙科診所看過牙醫，年幼時也都有讀過童詩。牙醫和詩人是很少有交集的兩種專業。但沙白（涂秀田牙醫師）卻能一手幫病人植牙，另一隻手執筆寫出生動的童詩，長期專注地耕耘，他在杏壇和「詩領域」，都散發出耀人的光芒。

沙白寫詩很早，就讀高雄醫學院時，就擔任阿米巴詩社的社長，也是心臟詩社、布穀鳥詩社的成員；他的詩集「太陽的流聲」、「星星亮晶晶」和「星星愛童詩」等，都曾被譯為日文、韓文，在外國的詩壇被廣為推介。

沙白的詩作受到肯定，他也多次受邀參加亞洲詩人大會、世界詩人大會，和世界華文兒童文學筆會等。

沙白的三本兒童詩集「星星亮晶晶」、「星星愛童詩」、「唱歌的河流」，其內容均經國立高雄師範大學前英語所所長暨文學院院長陳靖奇教授翻譯成英文，可中英對照閱讀，是兒童雙語文學的優良讀物，特此推薦。

南投縣長 林明溱 謹識

Everybody has visited a dentist and read children's poetry, but dentistry and children's mixed together are rarely seen. Sar Po (Dr. Shiu-tien Tu) can treat his patients' teeth with one hand and write children's poetry with the other. Having written prose and poetry for a long time, he is well known to all.

Sar Po began to write poetry at an early age when he was studying at Kaohsiung Medical University. There he was a member of the following clubs of poetry: The Amoeba Club of Poetry (where he used to serve as its President), The Heart Club of Poetry and The Cuckoo Club of Poetry. Some of his poems in the three collections of his children's poetry, Twinkle, Twinkle, Little Stars, Stars Love Children's Poetry and Singing Rivers, were translated into Japanese and Korean. They are welcome overseas.

He received acclaims from everywhere. He was invited to attend The Asian Congress for Poets, The World Congress for Poets, and the World Congress for Children's Literature in Chinese many times.

The three collections of his children's poetry, Twinkle, Twinkle, Little Stars, Stars Love Children's Poetry and Singing Rivers, will be published with their Chinese and English texts. The English rendition was done by Ching-chi Chen, Ph.d., Professor Emeritus of English, formerly Dean of Liberal Arts, National Kaohsiung Normal University. I believe that our children will benefit from the reading of them.

Knowing that their publication would be good for education of our students / pupils, I strongly recommend them to our teachers and parents.

> Mingzhen Lin (林明溱)
> Magistrate, Nantou County, Taiwan,
> Republic of China.

Penghu County Government

澎湖縣政府

涂院長秀田勛鑒

涂院長醫學揚名國際，文學創作豐碩，文壇譽為「國際海洋詩人」。「星星愛童詩」、「星星亮晶晶」、「唱歌的河流」等三本童詩，是我國兒童文學珍貴資產。今與高師大陳靖奇教授合作，將純真雋永的詩篇，編印華、英雙語推廣，令人敬佩。編印之際，謹祝發揚光大，世界看見臺灣兒童文學之美。

祝福您與家人平安健康。

澎湖縣 縣長
賴峰偉 謹上
110 年 5 月 21 日

澎湖縣馬公市治平路32號
32 Chihping RD, Makung Penghu, Taiwan R.O.C
Tel:886-6-9272300 Fax:886-6-9264060

Dear Dr. Shiu-tien Tu,

Your being an expert in dentistry and having written extensively in prose and poetry have helped establish your reputation as a renowned dentist and an international poet. Your three collections of children's poetry, Twinkle, Twinkle, Little Stars, Stars Love Children's Poetry and Singing Rivers, to be published with their Chinese and English texts can be an asset to our education. The English rendition done by Ching-chi Chen, Ph.d., Professor Emeritus of English, National Kaohsiung Normal University, would help the students to enjoy the beauty of poetry and to learn English for their daily life. I believe that our children will benefit from the reading of them in their enjoyment of Taiwan's children's literature and learning of English.

With best regards, I remain
Sincerely yours,
Feng-wui Lai (賴峰偉),
Magistrate, Penghu County, Taiwan,
Republic of China.
May 21, 2021.

邁出了第二步
——談沙白的人和詩

沙白是學醫的，但是他更喜歡兒童文學工作者成了朋友。沙白寫作勤，除了經常為報紙、雜誌撰稿以外，在文學創作方面寫得多的是新詩。他愛上了兒童文學以後，很自然的也為孩子寫了不少的詩。去年，他把他為孩子寫的詩編成一個集子「星星亮晶晶」，這是他向兒童詩邁出的第一步。今年，他又把一年來為孩子寫的詩編成第二個集子「星星愛童詩」。這是他向兒童詩邁出的第二步。沙白天性爽朗，再加上意識到他的讀者是小孩子，所以他寫的詩都很明朗。例如他寫的「河流」，就有這樣的特色：

我是一條喜歡旅行的河流

從上游到下游

從山上游到海口

轉了千個彎

唱了萬首歌

日日夜夜流

他既然已經喜歡上了兒童詩，自然會繼續走下去，「深入蠻荒」，尋找屬於他自己的綠洲，他很謙虛，承認他為兒童寫的詩是一種嘗試。其實，那就是他對兒童詩的探索。

林良

16

一個寫兒童詩的人，難免接觸到一些「兒童詩論」。沙白曾經談起：這些詩論大大困擾了他。我想，這是他求好心切的緣故。

詩論的作者，在詩論裏表達了他對「詩」的見識。詩論的多樣化，提高了「詩論領域」的價值。閱讀詩論可以增長我們對「詩」的見識。詩論的可讀，就在詩論作者的各說各話。就因為詩論作者的各說各話，才能對我們的創作產生一些刺激作用。如果天下的詩論竟出現空前的一致，甚至出現了範本，那麼一切創作就都將停工。

我們的小學裏，因為有「童詩教學」活動，在教學過程上不能沒有一定的「秩序」，所以無法避免採用比較科學的態度來處理童詩。童詩必須有「定義」，包括它的性質、形式、內容。一首詩的是不是童詩，要有嚴格的規定。一首詩的好壞，要有明確的立即判斷的標準。以這樣的立場寫出來的詩論，對創作者來說，讀起來當然更是「怕怕」。

購買的先決條件是必須有我們所要的貨品。如果沒有，就只好先放下購買意願，鼓勵製造。我們的童詩世界，目前最需要的是對創作的鼓勵，而不是對創作的「管理」。創作要有良好的環境。

良好的環境不是指一間安靜的房間，而是指一種期待的氣氛。一個人寫了一千首詩，其中只要有一首是你所喜愛的，就立刻介紹給廣大的讀者欣賞。期待要有恆不變，對作者要愛護。慢慢的，我們也就能有好詩「三百首」了。

期待的氣氛不是：一個人剛開始寫了第一首詩，令你失望，就兇狠狠的把他罵回去。

17

純淨可愛的詩論，其實也並不困擾人；不但不困擾，反而對創作者有幫助。沙白讀得較多而感到困擾的是可怕的「詩罵」。我很希望擅長寫「詩罵」的人，換一種稿紙，靜下心來依自己的主張多從事創作，多為孩子寫幾首可讀的好詩。

以我國現在兒童詩的總成績來說，自己多種些好花，而且越種越多，總比罵別人小園裏種的都是野草，扛着鋤頭到處巡視，到處剷除好得多。詩的大地是無比的廣濶。

我對沙白說：好詩是歲月和智慧的結晶。對詩，旣要朝朝暮暮，也要天長地久。希望我們彼此對對方都有一份期待。你的勤於探索，使我相信你會比我更早找到你自己的綠洲。

（序文作者為中華民國兒童文學會理事長）

七十六年九月五日在台北

Marching out the Second Step:
a Discussion of Sar Po, the Man and His Poetry

──**Foreword by Lin Liang**

Sar Po majored in dentistry, yet he is also interested in children and literature. That is why he has made friends with people working in the field of literature. He has produced a lot of works and had them published in newspapers and magazines. Among the works, poetry, both new and children's, constitutes the majority. Loving children, he wrote poetry for them. The first collection of children's poetry is entitled, Twinkle, Twinkle, Little Stars. Now, the second collection, Stars Love Children's Poetry, is here with us. That is why I call it marching out the second step.

Sar Po is an open-minded person and, knowing that he is writing poetry for children, his poetry is easy to read. He describes the river as follows:

I am a river who likes to travel,
From up-streams to down-streams, and
From the mountains to the sea.
I make hundreds upon hundreds of turns and
Sing thousands upon thousands of songs,
Day and night.

I believe that, loving children's poetry, he would continue to write more. Marching into the wilds, he would find his oasis. He is humble in saying that writing children's poetry is only a new try. In truth, he is exploring a terra incognito.

To write children's poetry, he has read some poetics on it. Oftentimes, he said that poetics on children's poetry had puzzled him. I believe that the puzzlement is a sign of his desiring to write better poetry.

It seems to me that a writer on his own poetics has his own view of poetry writing. Reading poetics on children's poetry would of course enhance our view on it, but different theories on its writing could sometimes be conflicting. Indeed, different views could offer us different ideas on children's poetry. If all views are the same and unified, there would be no need to write more poetry.

In our primary schools, we have the course, Reading of Children's Poetry. There should be a definitive form of the course. We could not avoid applying some scientific approaches toward the teaching. In the teaching of children's poetry, the elements of the course are as follows: its nature, its form and its content. Whether or not a poem is a children's poem, there is a strict definition. Regrettably, poetry that meets the above-mentioned qualities would be something unwelcome to the writers.

In shopping for goods, we purchase the ones that satisfy our demand. If there is none in the market, we may turn to the production of new goods that satisfy our needs. In the same manner, we may write children's poetry that can satisfy our needs in the classroom. At present, what we need should be encouragement to write good children's poetry, not trying to administer its writing according to the rules set by any authority. In short, what we need is a good environment where poetry can be produced.

A good environment is not one that just offers a quiet space, but an atmosphere where we may anticipate something good and suitable for the writing of poetry. In an atmosphere where such anticipation occurs, the poet may compose a thousand pieces of poetry, only one of which may be to the liking of the readers. This only one can be publicized and introduced to the general public. Feeling of anticipation should be there, and the poet should be encouraged. Little by little, poems produced can amount to as many as Three Hundred Poems of the Tang Dynasty.

In an atmosphere where anticipation occurs, a disappointing poem might be produced. We might negatively criticize its inadequacy according to rules we have set.

Frankly speaking, an acceptable poetics is not that horrible and puzzling. It might help the poet along in his writing. I know that many negatively criticize some of the poems by Sar Po. I wish that those who criticize would leave him alone and try to write poems themselves for the good of the children.

It seems to me that in the garden of children's poetry, we should plant more flowers. We should not claim that flowers planted by others might be weeds. We should not carry hoes everywhere trying to destroy flowers planted by others as weeds. The more flowers there are, the better. The Good Earth is immense and is able to contain all.

I would like to say to Sar Po that good poetry is a crystallization of time and wisdom. Poetry is about temporariness and eternity. We should hope him well. We believe that, ceaselessly exploring in the realm of poetry, he would find his oasis.

By Lin Liang, President of the Association of Children's Literature, Republic of China, September 1987.

童詩的奇葩
——序沙白童詩集「星星愛童詩」

沙白是詩人醫生，他開業牙科診所，每天診療病人以外的時間，大多在診所的櫃台上寫詩、寫文章，經常在報紙上發表文章。他不但寫了許多成人的新詩，也出版過兩本成人詩集，而且，最可貴的是他還保持着童心，寫了許多兒童詩。去年已出版令人讚賞的童詩集「星星亮晶晶」，現在又要出版第二本兒童詩集「星星愛童詩」，創作量可說極為豐富。其作品又極富童心、童趣、啟發性和教育性，對兒童文藝之培養，幫助極大。本人從事教育數十年，對兒童文學也極有興趣，因此，對同是兒童文學家的沙白，如同林之鳥，極為賞識。

沙白幼年卽習古詩，故有深厚的文學基礎。高中以後，卽對新詩發生興趣，到大學三年級，就已出版頗具份量的詩集，並負責校刊雜誌。雖然，他現在是個開業牙醫師，但是，仍然一面研究醫學，一面研究文學不輟，常在許多報紙和雜誌發表文章，並翻譯英日文學，故可說是學貫中西，具有精密的科學頭腦和深廣的文學修養。最近對高雄的文藝活動極為熱心，指導童詩之創作和朗誦，獲得極佳的評譽。

藝夏令營講師，以文學的方式薰陶學生，以文學的方式來啟迪學生，這樣，學生不但喜歡聽，而且，在無形中達到了極好的效果，一時之效，而文學潛默移化的功效，最為彰顯而永久。我常常用講故事的方式來啟迪學生，這樣，學生不但喜歡聽，而且，在無形中達到了極好的效果，數千年來，綿延不斷。而詩是文學的精髓，兒童詩亦然，所以，我國古代的民俗兒童詩歌，數千年來，綿延不斷，仍在民間流傳，歌詠不輟，現代詩歌和兒童詩歌更是蓬勃

許漢章

發展。

本人為了促進兒童文學之發展，在六年前就創立了高雄兒童文學寫作協會，接著三年前又有了中華民國兒童文學會之創立，在林良理事長和大家努力之下，使我國兒童文學有組織、有系統地向前邁進，現在已經有了輝煌的成果。沙白是會員之一，也是一位優秀的耕耘者，今將其作品源源發表出版對兒童文學有了具體的貢獻，這是本會的光榮，在我們的兒童文學界，多開出了一朵鮮麗的奇葩，願教育界人士、學生和文藝愛好者仔細玩味欣賞，必有收獲。

（序文作者為高雄市兒童文學寫作協會理事長、苓洲國小校長）

Wonderful work of children's poetry

── By Xu Hanzhang

As a dentist, Sar Po has to meet and treat his patients during the day. In his spare time, he kept writing poems and essays to be published in newspapers and magazines. He wrote poems for the general public and poems for children. He has been a diligent writer. In a short period of time, he has two collections of children's poetry published: Twinkle, Twinkle, Little Stars, published last year, and now Stars Love Children's Poetry.

As an educator in primary school for many decades, I am also interested in children's literature. I found that Sar Po's poems to be of interest to children in their content, educative value and enlightenment of life. As such, I share comradeship with my fellow children's writer, Sar Po. I am appreciative of his works.

As a young person, Sar Po was interested in Chinese poetic classics. He has been well equipped with a strong background of literature. On his graduation of senior school, he had written new poetry, and in his junior year in college, he had a big volume of poetic works published. In the same year, he began to edit a magazine. Right now, in spite of being a practicing dentist, he has done a lot of research in literature. He wrote essays on foreign writers and contributed them to newspapers and magazines. He also did some translation of world classics from foreign languages into Chinese. As a dentist, he is being scientific, and yet he is at the same time well versed in arts and literature. Furthermore, he is enthusiastic in some activities concerning arts and literature in the City of Kaohsiung. He serves as a tutor in the Summer Camp for arts and literature. There he advises students how to compose children's poetry and how to chant it. He has won acclaim from doing that.

It seems to me, the best way to educate students is through the reading of literary works. Discipline on the basis of warning, reprimand, or corporeal punishment would not do much good. Only through literature and its activities can we imperceptibly shape children's personality. The effect of the former is temporary and may be detrimental to the children's personality, and that of the latter would last longer into the later phases of their life. I used to tell stories to enlighten the students to some basic ideas about life. They liked to hear the stories and they might learn lessons hinted in them.

Poetry seems to be the essence of literature, which is also true of children's poetry. In traditional Chinese society, poetry has been a vehicle carrying cultural values through generations. Poetic chanting has been a social activity amidst the general public. In our own time, modern poetry and children's poetry are also flourishing.

To promote children's literature, six years ago, I founded the Kaohsiung Children's Literature Writing Association. Then, three years ago, the Republic of China Association of Children's Literature was established. Under the leadership of Lin Liang and others, the progress of children's literature is heading toward a fruitful future. Sar Po is one of the committee members of the Association. He is a good tiller in the field of children's literature. He has done much in the field through producing a lot of works. In the field, we need more people to contribute more works for the students, the educators and the general public.

—Xu Hanzhang (許漢章), Principal, Lingzhou Primary School,
　and President, the Kaohsiung Children's Literature Writing Association.

〈返回童年時光隧道的作家──沙白〉 ◎藍芸（作家‧詩人）

國際詩人沙白老師，近期欲將他早期出版過的童詩，《星星愛童詩》、《唱歌的河流》及《星星亮晶晶》做英文翻譯。排版成中英文對照本，重新印刷成新版本。前中華民國文學學會理事長林良先生曾說過「我對沙白說：好詩是歲月和智慧的結晶。對詩，既要朝朝暮暮，也要天長地久。」曾任高雄市和台北市教育局的毛連塭局長，在他的童詩出版寫序文時，對其童詩作品亦有多方讚賞！

愛詩者，除了要心思細膩敏銳，更要恆心毅力，才能在不斷的寫作經歷中，「去蕪存菁」，端出更優良作品。沙白老師的童詩曾在許多個報紙、詩刊…及多所小學刊物上登過。和我們小學時最親密的「國語日報」也刊過不少。如：1990年5月參加大陸湖南所舉辦的「世界華文兒童文學筆會」，發表的論文「兒童詩的探索」就刊於79年5月31日的國語日報上。

拜讀過沙白老師的童詩後，真訝異這是一位中年詩人所寫出的童真詩作！一個詩人所具備的細膩心思、敏銳觀察力；對兒童的天真心靈，直敘不造作的思維，都能掌握精準！若不是書上寫著「沙白著作」，真讓人以為是那個天才小學生的優秀作品。

真佩服沙白老師的多元寫作功力！不但成人詩寫得好，具有國際觀，有對人生歷練的深刻體悟，深入淺出，卻意涵深遠，處處禪思哲理。現代詩裡有著後現代詩的超然意味，還有一點醫學專業素養，連兒童詩都寫得很吸睛！令人有頓時返回童年的時光隧道，走入童畫世界之感！

兒童的心靈很純真！天真浪漫，不經雕琢的言語，可能天馬行空，可能很突奇！但常是可以集成一首動人的詩歌。在現代的科技電腦世界裡，兒童的思維早已超乎我們所想像的聰慧！

老師在寫童詩時已然忘卻自己年齡，跟著家裡的孩子走進他們的世界裡融合一起，用心思考和觀察，才能有如此貼近兒童思維的傑作！加上貼切幽默感的插畫，不但吸引孩

26

童，連大人都喜歡！

童詩不一定是要兒童所寫的，成人帶著一顆純真童語，還有一點對人生觀察體悟的角度和想像力！如：《星星亮晶晶》裡的〈蠟燭〉，……請別自卑！小小的針頭，可以麻醉獅子；小小的子彈，可以殺死大象；星星之火，可以燎原。還有〈露〉的第一行「露珠像情人的眼淚」；大概還沒有兒童能成熟到有如此豐富的「想像力」！

《唱歌的河流》裡〈星星和螢火蟲〉星星一閃一閃亮晶晶／螢火蟲一閃一閃比美麗／星星在天上發信號／螢火蟲在地上通信息／他們相互交談遊戲／並探求宇宙的秘密／請我們去解謎。哈哈！這麼富有科技性聯想力的「童詩」！

〈唱歌的河流〉這名字給人許多想像！很浪漫，很詩情！河流會隨著氣候和水量的變化不同，唱著有「抑揚頓挫」不同旋律的歌曲；時而輕柔慢流，也會有滾滾河沙澎湃洶湧的高亢節奏，如演奏一首「交響樂曲」般的旋律。

沙白老師寫〈唱歌的河流〉河流是流浪的歌手／從山上流到海口／一面旅行一面唱歌／他是快樂的歌手。想像一下，河流真的很像一個瀟灑又自在的歌手，從高山流經平地而入大海，日以繼夜，悠悠流著，唱著。

《星星愛童詩》裡的〈溫度計〉溫度計是感情豐富的升降機／熱的時候高興升起／冷的時候低頭縮頸／像小妹妹的脾氣。這個比喻真貼切又逗趣！真的，小孩子鬧脾氣時的情緒，就像支溫度計。

〈湍流〉考試時／就像游泳於湍流中／要先有平時訓練的良好技術／才能得高分。這是首富有教育性的小詩，平時不努力用功，臨時抱佛腳，是得不到好成績的。

沙白老師的心思縝密，寫詩真的很用心！一本優良的童詩對兒童具有啟迪智慧，延伸想像力作用，是開啟兒童心靈的最佳鑰匙，也是教育兒童的最佳讀物。

拜讀過沙白老師的童詩及其他作品後，讓我有不同的深刻領略，對詩有著更宏觀的「視」界！他的作品老少咸宜，不但具有教育意義，又充滿豐富想像力，尤其是對兒童或青少年更有啟迪作用，為兒童開闢一片翠綠「詩」園地！是很值得推廣的優良作品。

An Author Returning to Childhood Days through a Time Tunnel

—藍芸Lan Yun

At present, internationally known poet, Sar Po, is trying to have his three collections of children's poetry, translated into English. They are Twinkle, Twinkle, Little Stars, The Singing Rivers and The Stars Love Children's Poetry. In the new editions, texts, English and Chinese, will be set side by side.

His poetry has been widely accepted. Former President of the Republic of China Children's Literature Association, Lin Liang, said, "I told Sar Po that good poetry is a crystallization of time and intelligence. Poetry should be of temporariness and of eternity." Former Commissioner of Education, Kaohsiung and Taipei Cities respectively, Mao Lianwen, praises Sar Po's children's poetry in his "Forward" to the latter's collection, Twinkle, Twinkle, Little Stars.

A good poet should be able to observe keenly things around him with an untiring attitude and to write continuously in order that "Practice makes perfect." Sar Po's poetry has been published in many newspapers and magazines including the Guoyu Newspaper most loved by children. In May 1990, he read a paper, "On Children's Poetry," at the PEN International Congress for Children's Literature in Hunan Province, Mainland China. The paper was published in the Guoyu Newspaper in May 31, 1990.

After having read Sar Po's poetry, I was surprised at finding how a middle-aged poet could write such works as contained children's innocence. He was well equipped with the power of keen observation and minute deliberation of the pure mind of children. He was good at grasping it and expressing it in images easy to understand. The poems seem to have been written by some gifted children poets, not by an adult one.

Truly, I admire Sar Po in his multiple capabilities. He writes poetry for the general public. Its topics are widely ranged: international affairs, those between the two sides of the Taiwan Strait, those about interpersonal relations, those of society and nation, etc. His poetry is philosophical with Chan (Zen) Buddhism in it, modern poetry with colors of postmodernism in it. I also find some medical knowledge and that of science and technique in his poetry. His children's poetry catches the eye of the young readers. Reading his children's poetry, one seems to be able to travel back to one's childhood days through an imaginary time machine.

Children's mind could be like a sheet of white paper. Being pure and innocent, children could be outlandish or out of touch with reality in their use of language. Indeed, their speeches could be put together to form poetry. In the virtual domain of our information society, however, children seem to be well talented in their imagination and use of language.

Writing his children's poetry, Sar Po seems to have forgotten his own age. Together with his own children, he wanders in the poetic world. With children's mind, he writes poetry to share with his readers, children and adults alike, his keen and humous observation of things in that world.

Children's poetry could be written by an adult if he still retains children's mind. He sees the world in children's intelligence. In the poem, "The Candle," in Twinkle,Twinkle, Little Stars, he advises the needle point not to belittle itself because it could etherize a big lion; in the same manner, a little bullet could kill a gigantic elephant, and a little spark of fire could blaze a huge pasture. In the first line in "Dew," he writes, "dew is like lovers' tears." It seems to me that few children could be mature enough to have worked out such comparisons. The poem, "Little Stars and Fireflies," in the collection of The Singing River, says that

> Bright little stars
> Are vying with the fireflies in their brilliancy.
> It seems that the stars up in the sky are giving off messages
> For the fireflies to receive on earth.
> They are communicating
> And are together trying to reveal the secret of the universe.

In this children's poem, we find elements of science fiction calling children's attention to something that might happen in the universe.

The title of the poem,"The Singing River," allows us to think of some romantic and poetic images. In different seasons, the volume of water in the river would determine the manner and sound of its singing giving different musical movements, being adagio, andante, moderato, allegro, etc. Sometimes, during the deluge of the river, the music can be loud and threatening giving an image of a symphony of destiny. Furthermore, the singing river is compared to a lone and wandering singer singing all the way from upstreams down to the plains and finally to the sea.

In the poem, "The Thermometer," in The Stars Love Children's Poetry, the thermometer is compared to "An elevator of passion / When hot, it rises happily, / And when cold, it shrinks / Like a finicky little girl." The comparison is apt and interesting. Indeed, little children's passion is exactly like one described about the thermometer above.

In "Turbulent Currents," taking examinations is "Like swimming in turbulent currents. / One has to do a lot of practice in order to be skillful in managing them and to gain high scores." Practice makes perfect as the saying goes.

Sar Po has taken pains in the writing of the poems. Good children's poetry can be enlightening, and it allows the readers to think of a lot of others things. The poetry offers them a key to a new world.

Having read the three collections of children's poetry by Sar Po, I come to an understanding; his poetry helps open up a new perspective of one's vision. His poetry is educative and full of imagination. It is like a green garden, and reading it is good for readers of all ages.

自序

兒童的心靈清新純潔，兒童對這個世界懷著無限的好奇、趣味和幻想。法國名作家米修・突尼耶認為只有孩童，才可以帶領我們「重新回到最基本的樂趣和事實」。

一九七八年諾貝爾文學獎得主辛格，也是一個兒童文學家，當他在接受諾貝爾文學獎時，很特別地，以「我為什麼要替孩子寫作？」為演講詞的題目，他說：「只要是涉及的是真正的文學，兒童便是最佳的讀者。……當成人文學如江水東流似的消逝時，許久之後，為兒童而寫的書籍，將是作品、邏輯和信念的最後堡壘，使人們相信家庭、神、還有真正的人道主義。……在我們這個年代，當成人文學日走下坡的時候，上乘的兒童文學便是唯一的希望，唯一的安庇所。」可見兒童文學，不僅是屬於兒童的東西，而且，也是人類最原始的、最基本的、最純潔的靈魂的故鄉和聖地。

童詩是捕捉兒童心靈的最佳語言文字的工具，也是展現兒童心靈的美麗繪畫和優美的歌聲。

本人於去年出版兒童詩集「星星亮晶晶」之後，幸獲各界佳評，譬如，名詩人林清泉於國語日報專評推介，名作家吳燈山也曾在中國語文專評推崇此書。某大作家曾評為：「語言輕快活潑，有節奏感。想像豐富、天真有趣有啟發性也有空靈的意境。」而這第二本兒童詩集「星星愛童詩」的風格，也和第一本相近，全部是今年寫的作品，有些曾發表於國語日報、台灣新生報、台灣時報、新聞晚報、滿天星詩刊和秋水詩刊等。

我的童詩有些適宜朗誦，譬如，名朗誦家白原朗誦過，「春天」曾經

沙白

32

我覺得兒童詩，應以精簡為妙，不一定非要用楊喚等人的長長的童話詩的風格不可，也就是說，詩最好是以最精短的詩語和最清新的意象，來表現最精純的詩味，才是上乘。譬如，李白的「靜夜思」：「床前明月光，疑是地上霜，舉頭望明月，低頭思故鄉。」用字那麼明白淺易，只有短短的二十個字，給人感動的程度，遠超過用了許多難字而長達八百四十字的白居易的「長恨歌」。可見，長詩或長的童話詩，只是童詩的一種形式而已，並不是每一個人都非寫這種形式的童詩不可。

有人概略地把「兒童詩」定義為「兒童寫的詩」和「給兒童讀的詩」及「適合兒童欣賞的詩」等，我却將之深入定義為：「具有兒童靈魂及兒童意識的詩。也就是在感覺和知覺上，對事物及其意象之表現，容易為兒童心靈感應的詩。」有人問我為什麼要寫兒童詩？我說是「詩言志」，也就是用詩來表達我所想的一切。我寫的成人詩，有些是寫實的，有些是超現實的，都是為了表達我的心靈之所思、所欲、感覺、知覺和理想，寫兒童詩又為了表達純真的童心和回歸兒童心靈的故鄉。

保羅・梵樂希說：「詩是體驗的表現，詩人的目的，乃在於讀者作心靈的共鳴，和讀者共享神聖的一刻。」寫成人詩之目的如此，寫兒童詩亦然；也就是，以自己的童心來和兒童作心靈的共鳴，並和兒童共享愉快有趣的、神聖的一刻。

我希望本詩集，能夠像另一顆小星星，閃耀在兒童文學的天空裡，引起大家欣賞的樂趣。

在高雄文化中心朗誦過。有些詩也有兒歌的味道。

Preface

—Sar Po.

Children's mind could be like a sheet of blank, pure paper. They are curious about the world around them. According to a renowned French author, it is only children who can lead us back to revisit the most fundamental facts and pleasure of our life.

The 1978 Nobel Laureate for Literature, Isaac Bashevis Singer (Yiddish: יצחק רעגניז סיוועשאַב; November 11, 1903 – July 24, 1991), also a writer in children's literature, made the his speech in his acceptation ceremony of the title, "Why I wrote for children?" He said, "Anything concerning children can be true literature. Children could be good readers. When literary works for the adults vanish like river water flowing into the sea, some good children's literature would remain and become the last bulwark and shelter for our culture." Indeed, children's literature does not belong to children only. It is the home and a holy place for the purest, the most original, and the most fundamental soul in the world." Children's poetry employs the best language to capture children's soul, beautiful mind, and melodious voices.

Last year, I had my first collection, Twinkle, Twinkle, Little Stars, published, and it has received positive criticism from all circles. Lin Qingquan, a renowned poet, introduced the collection and wrote an essay about it in the Guoyu Newspaper. Wu Dengshan, a writer, wrote an essay in The Chinese Language and Literature to recommend it to the public with high esteem. Still another writer commented, "The language in Twinkle, Twinkle, Little Stars is lively and rhythmic. The poems are rich in imagination. They are about children's innocence and illumination of children's innate soul." Moreover, the present collection, Stars Love Children's Poetry, shares the similar style with the first. All the poems were written during the past year; some were published in the Guoyu Newspaper, the Taiwan Xinsheng Newspaper, the Taiwan Times, the Evening News Post, the Mantianxing Journal for Poetry, and the Qiushui Journal for Poetry.

Some of the poems can be chanted. Bai Yuan, a well-known chanter, did the chanting of "Springtime" at Kaohsiung Cultural Center. Others are like nursery rhymes.

It seems to me that children's poetry should be simple and easy to understand. I don't agree with Yang Huan in that he insists that it should be long poems about fairy tales. In other words, in children's poetry, simple and concise words and clear images should be used to express the purest emotions. In Li Po's "A Quiet Night Thought," he says,

In front of my bed there is bright moonlight,
It looks as if it were frost on the ground.
I lift my head and gaze at the August moon;
I lower my head and think of my hometown.

In the poem, words simple and easy to understand are used. There are only twenty Chinese words in the poem. I would like to say that the poem far excels Bai Juyi's "Song of Everlasting Sorrow" which is a long poem with difficult words and intricate images. In Bai's poem, there are 840 Chinese words. Poems can be short and long. We should not expect that all good poems should be long ones.

Children's poetry can be defined as follows: Poetry written by children, poetry written for children and poetry fit for children. However, I would like to define it: Poetry that has children's soul and that which appeals to children as its content in being able to touch children emotionally and intellectually through concrete images and cognition of things around them. Some might ask me why I write children's poetry. Poetry expresses one's will; that is to say, I write poetry to express my intentions and thoughts about life. I write poems for adults and for children. Some of my poems for adults are realistic and others, surrealistic. They all express what I think, what I desire, what I feel and am conscious of, and what I think that things ought to be. The poems I write for children are those about the children's mind, and they would bring us back to the homeland of children's spirit.

Paul Valery says, "Poetry is about the poet's experience. It aims at the reader's resonance of the spirit and shares with him a holy moment of life." The same can be true of poetry for adults and for children. To write poetry for children, we should be equipped with children's mind, so we can gain their responses and share with them their happiness, pleasure and the holy moment.

I wish that the present collection would be like a star in the sky of children's literature and give the readers the pleasure of reading.

●昨天五月四日是文藝節，也是牙醫師節。對喜愛從事現代詩創作的牙醫師涂秀田而言，昨天白天他在診所為病人治療牙疾，晚上則赴高雄中正文化中心參加文藝活動朗誦自己的詩篇，度過忙碌又快樂的一天。

提起涂秀田，知道他的人不多；但若說出他的筆名「沙白」，喜歡現代詩的朋友大概就知道他了。

一如他的本名，涂秀田來自屏東縣竹田鄉的農村，高雄醫學院牙醫系畢業，並曾留學日本東京大學，現在高雄市自行開業牙科診所。不少人對牙科多少都有點畏懼感，覺得牙科診所內不外是冷冷硬硬的器械，難以拿來跟轉折迭宕的現代詩聯想在一起。

「牙醫師和詩人的雙重身分並不衝突，反倒是相輔相成。」「沙白」指出，因為每天面對不同職業的病人，他可以觀察社會各層面的眾生，激發更多的靈感，找出更生活化的題材。在高醫念書時，涂秀田曾任校內阿米巴詩社社長，後來也擔任過南杏雜誌社社長，先後出版過詩集「河品」及「太陽的流聲」。留日歸國後，沙白也努力從事翻譯國際詩人的名作，散見國內各報章。

九年前開始，他有了子女，也發現人世最美的真情——童心，他開始朝童詩方面拓展藝術

牙醫詩人最快樂的一天
涂秀田 歡度雙重佳節

本報記者 殷延泉

的領域。

一首「蜻蜓」，如是寫著：「你是一隻漂亮的小飛機／在河邊草上飛來飛去／你跟我們捉迷藏／哈！哈！好有趣／請問你為什麼不必加汽油／也能飛得那麼久？」

沙白更精確的抓住兒童心理，活潑的寫出了「鼻子會唱歌」，同時也傳達了醫藥保健常識及父母關愛之情。

「我的鼻子會唱歌。」小弟說：「為什麼我的鼻子會唱歌？」媽媽說：「你唱的是感冒鼻塞歌。」／小弟問：「你冬天穿得單薄，玩水玩得太多。以後再這樣子，竹鞭也會咻咻唱歌。」／小弟說：「我不敢再這樣子了。」

沙白今年四十三歲，每天在病人治疾之餘，坐在窄小的寫字檯前，仍埋首企圖寫下自腦海一閃即逝的每一個聲音。

去年，他參加漢城的國際詩人大會，發表了「珊瑚礁」一首詩，其中的句子，似可說明沙白對詩的執著：

「而珊瑚礁是一首寫不完的詩／昨天寫過了／今天還寫著／明天還繼續寫⋯⋯」

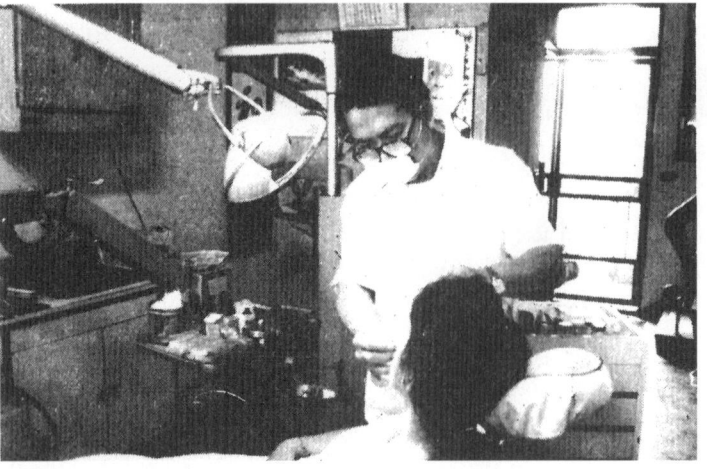

牙醫師涂秀田也是一位詩人。（本報記者 殷延泉攝）

The Happiest Day for Dr. Tu Shiu-tien

Yesterday, May Fourth, was a Festival for Arts and Literature. It was also a Physician's Day. For Dr. Tu, it was a double festival. During the day, he had to treat his patients in his clinic, and at evening he had to rush to Kaohsiung Chiang Kai-shek Cultural Center to attend an activity for arts and literature to read his poems. Dr. Tu was busy and happy the whole day.

The name of Tu Shiu-tien may not be well-known to all, but his nom de plume, Sar Po, is familiar to many who like modern poetry.

Dr. Tu is from Zhutian Township, Pingdong. He earned a Bachelor's degree from Kaohsiung Medical College and pursued further studies at National University of Tokyo. Right now, he owns a dental clinic and works there as a dentist.

Many people are afraid of dentists and think that dentists' tools and machines in the clinic might be cold and lifeless. It is difficult to associate them to modern poetry.

Sar Po says that being a dentist and being a poet are not conflicting. In actuality, they may be complementary. Every day when he treats the patients who are from all walks of life, he talks with them about their experiences of life. From the talks with and the observation of them, he gains inspiration for his poetry.

In college, he used to serve as President of the Amoeba Society for Poetry, and later he served as President of the Nanxing Magazine. He had his works, Hepin and the Flowing Sounds of the Sun, published.

After returning from Japan to Taiwan, he did translation of some world-famous foreign poets. The translation can be found in many magazines and newspapers.

Nine years ago, his children were born. In them, he found the most beautiful passion in the world— children's mind. The beauty ignited the spark of his interest in the realm of children's poetry and he began to explore the newfound land.

In the poem, "The Dragonfly," he writes,
You are a little, pretty airplane
Flying here and there over the meadow near the river.
You are playing hide-and-seek with us.
Ha, ha, ha, it's interesting.
Why can you fly for so long a time
Without any gasoline?"

Sar Po is able to grasp the mind of children. In "The Nose that Sings," he interestingly combines medical knowledge with parental love:

My little brother says, "My nose can sing.
Mother says, "You are singing the song of a stuffed nose."
My little brother asks, "Why does my nose sing?"
Mother says "In winter, your clothing is not enough and
You have been playing with water.
If you keep doing it,
I believe that the bamboo stick in my hand would sing, too."
My little brother says, "OK, I would not do it again in the future."

Sar Po is forty-three years old now. In his spare time, he writes poems at the narrow desk in his clinic. He tries to capture the fleeting moments of his poetic inspiration in his mind there.

Last year, he went to Seoul, Korea, to attend the World Congress for Poets. There, he read his poem, "A Coral reef Is a Poem," in which we can see his undying passion for the writing of poetry:

I shall never get tired of writing about a coral reef which is a poem and of which
I wrote yesterday,
I am still writing today, and
I shall be writing tomorrow.

—Yin Yanquan, the Minsheng Newspaper, May 5, 1987.

月亮和星星

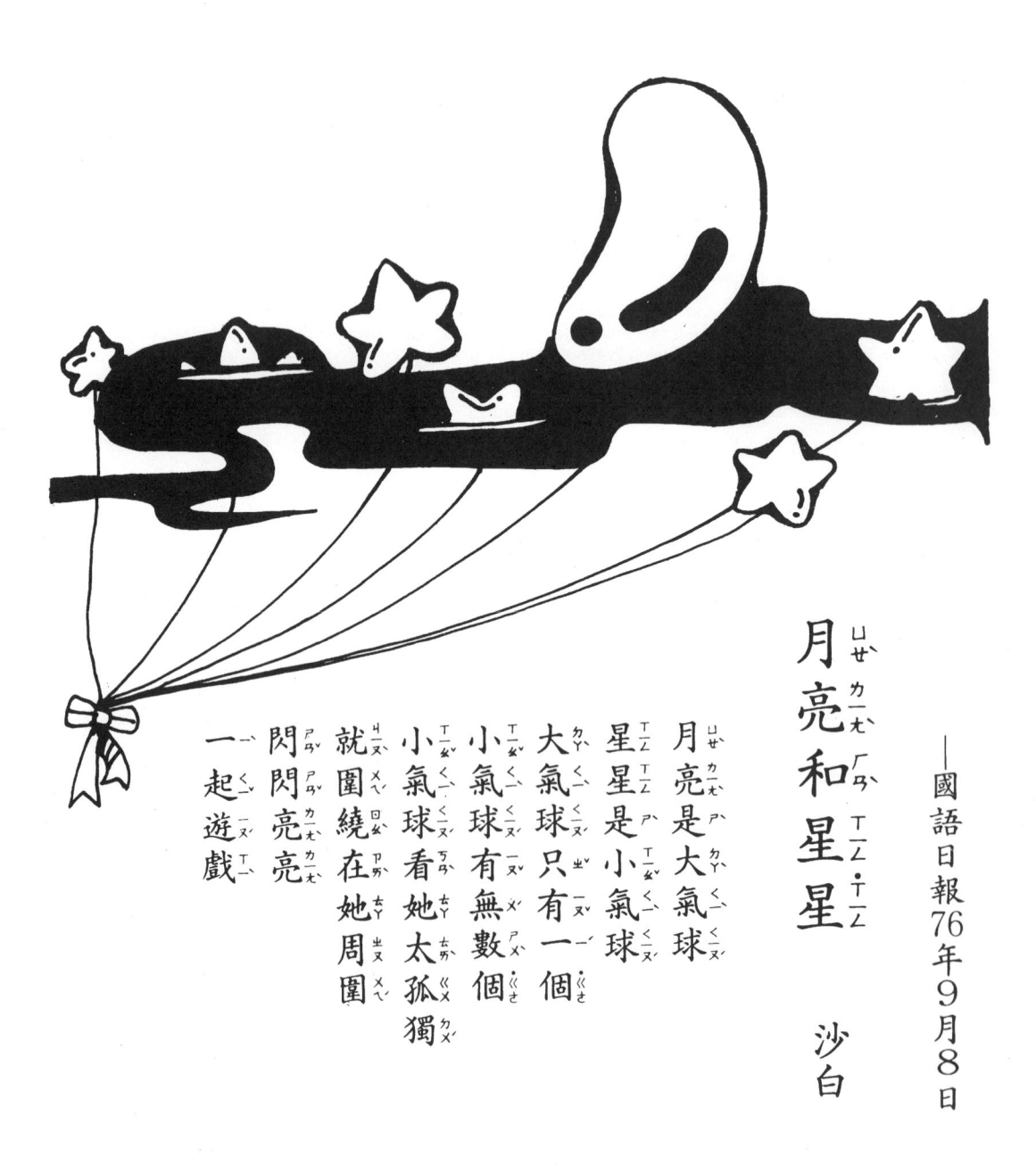

沙白

月亮是大氣球
星星是小氣球
大氣球只有一個
小氣球有無數個
小氣球看她太孤獨
就圍繞在她周圍
閃閃亮亮
一起遊戲

——國語日報76年9月8日

The Moon and the Stars

The moon is like a big balloon, and
The stars, small ones.
There is one big balloon, and
There are countless small ones.
The big one is lonely, so
The small ones surround it,
Blinking and
Playing around it.

— Guoyu Daily, September 8, 1987.

太陽月亮星星

沙白

太陽月亮星星
像自動自發的太空人
以共同的語言
互報信息旅行
他們互相尊重
保持距離
而不撞擊
希望我們的司機
這樣保持距離行駛

The Sun, the Moon and the Stars

The sun, the moon and the stars are
Like self-luminous astronauts.
They communicate with a common language
To tell how each travels in space.
They have come to a consensus:
They keep safe distances from one another
So that they would not bump into one another.
It is my hope that our earthly drivers
Would also keep safe distances on our highways.

星星和太陽　　白沙

在天空裡
快樂的小星星們
拿着電燈在遊戲
整夜不睡
太陽起床後
就把他們趕走
星星又出來
而太陽下山睡覺時
在天上遊戲
天天如此
年年如此
太陽永遠是爸爸
星星永遠是小孩
爸爸永遠管不完
小孩永遠玩不完

The Sun and the Stars

In the sky,
The happy little stars are
Holding electric light bulbs and playing.
They do not sleep all night.
The sun appears and
Drives them away.
When the sun goes down behind the mountains to sleep,
They appear again.
They again play happily in the sky,
Day in and day out,
Year in and year out.
It seems that the sun is the father, and
The stars, children.
Endlessly, the father tries to discipline the children.
Endlessly, the children tend to play all the time.

白沙　星星和太陽

在天空裡
快樂的小星星們
拿着小電燈在遊戲
整夜不睡
太陽起床後
就把他們趕走
而太陽下山睡覺時
星星又出來
在天上遊戲
天天如此
年年如此
永遠玩不膩
真有趣

The Sun and the Stars

In the sky,
Happy little stars are
Holding little electric light bulbs and playing.
They do not sleep all night.
The sun appears and
Drives them away.
When the sun goes down behind the mountains to sleep,
They appear again.
They again play happily in the sky,
Day in and day out,
Year in and year out.
It is fun to see that
They are never tired of playing.

太陽
星星
燈光

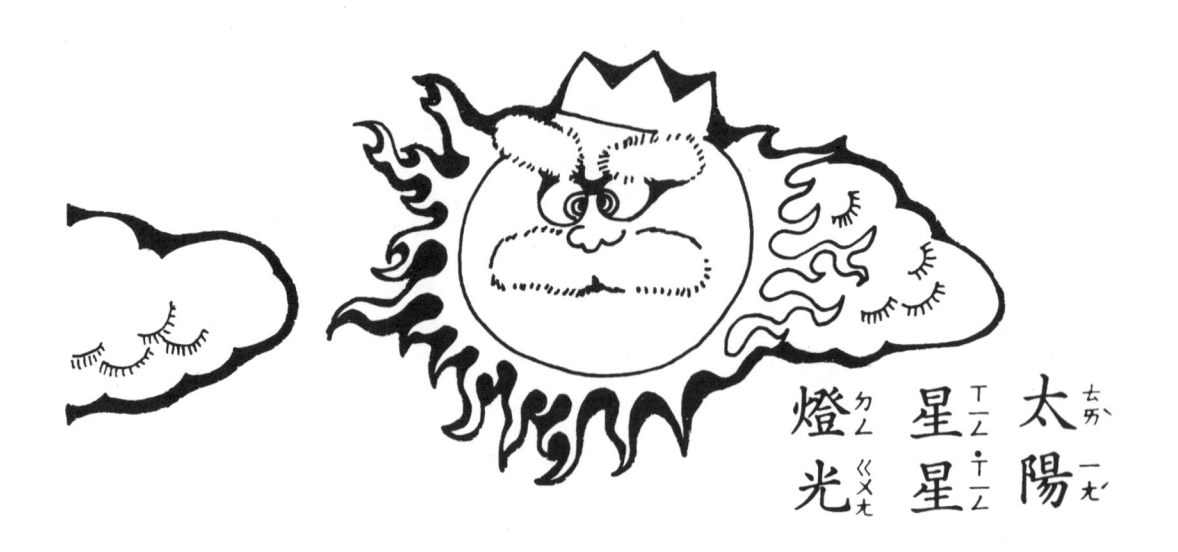

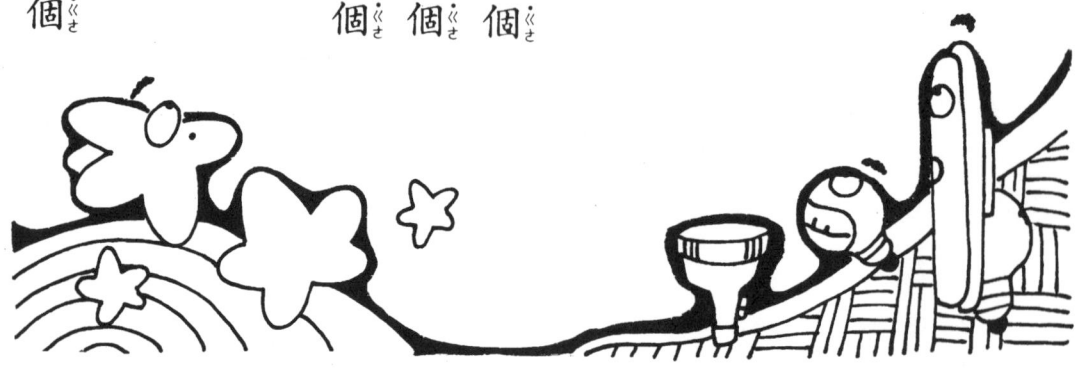

燈光小小
小小燈光
星星小小
小小星星
大太陽
太陽大
太陽大，只要一個
星星小，要無數個
燈光小，要許多個
太陽大，只要一個
偉大的只要一個
渺小的卻有無數個

The Sun, the Stars and Light Bulbs

Light bulbs are small.
Small are light bulbs.
The stars are small.
Small are the stars.
The sun is huge.
Huge is the sun.
The sun is huge, and we need only one.
Light bulbs are small, and we need a lot.
The stars are small, and we need more than a lot.
The sun is huge.
We need only a great one, and, however,
We need a lot of small ones.

太陽　沙白

太陽是最守時的照燈人
每天清晨打開巨燈
照耀我們
他不必領薪水
他很富有
比石油大王還富有
他的能力強過石油
他的光芒雄霸宇宙

新聞晚報76、6

The Sun

The sun is the most punctual light giver.
Every day in the morning he turns on a huge lantern
To give us light.
He doesn't need wages.
He is rich.
He is richer than petrol kings.
He is more powerful than petroleum.
His light tyrannizes the cosmos.

—Evening News Post, June 1987.

電燈

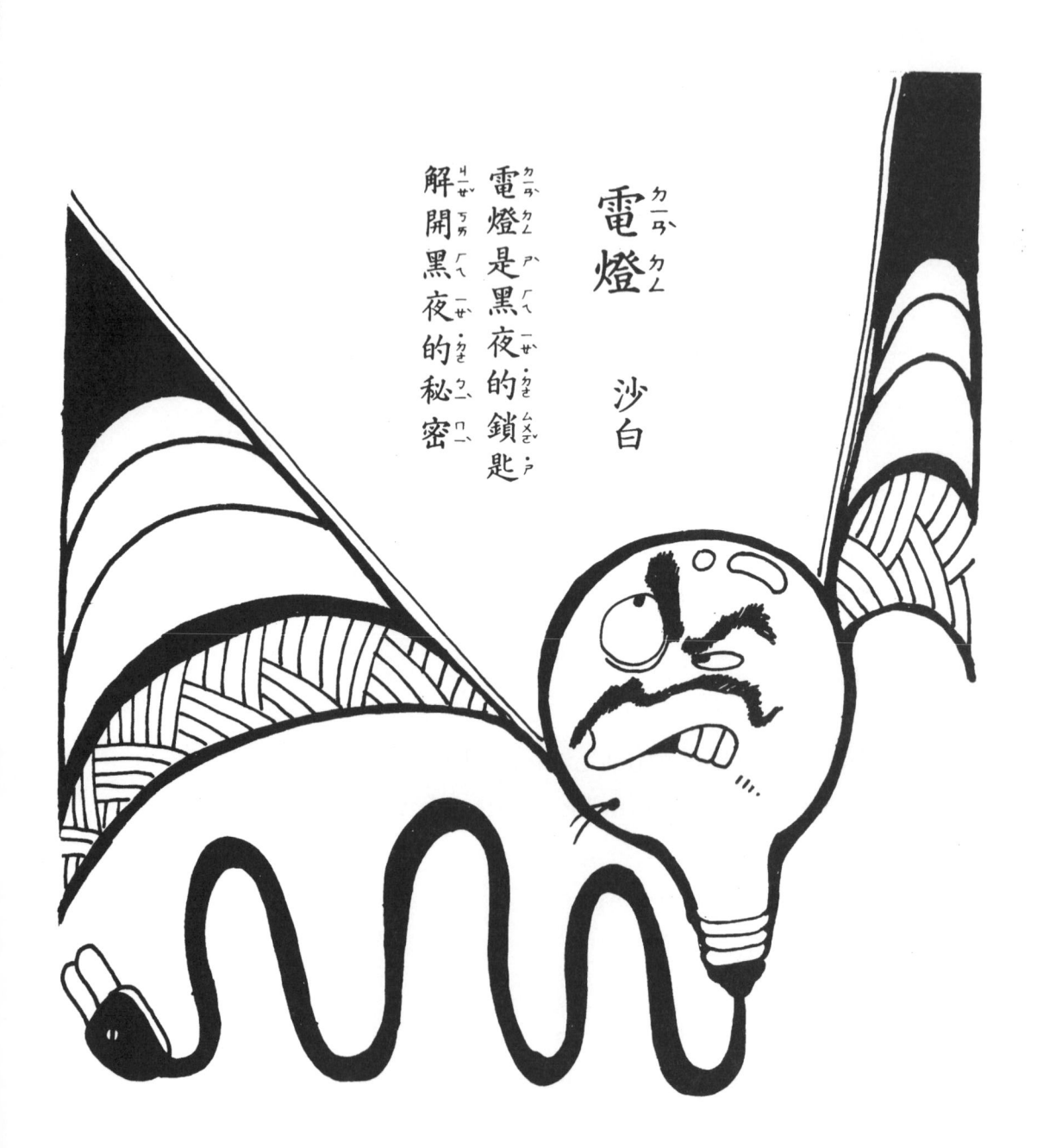

沙白

電燈是黑夜的鎖匙
解開黑夜的秘密

Light Bulbs

Light bulbs are keys
To unlock the secret of the black night.

黑夜　沙白

黑夜像多情的少女
拿着一塊巨大的黑布
遮住我們的眼睛和大地
在黑幕裡
做有趣的遊戲

The Black Night

The black night is like a passionate young lady.
She covers our eyes and the earth
With a gigantic black cloth.
Under it,
She does a lot of fun things there.

中秋月 沙白

一對小情侶曾在中秋月上
寫着金石盟的愛情
每次他們看見月亮
月亮就像電視一樣
放映金石盟的故事
給他們欣賞

The Mid-Autumn Moon

Two young lovers, at the night of the mid-autumn moon,
Wrote down their powerful love.
Every time when they see the moon, they will see the
    scenario of their love as if on television.
They will enjoy the scenario of their own strong love.

月夜

沙白

在夜之巨杯裡
月亮和星星
像粒粒蛋黃
懸浮在夜空的湯裡
閃耀着

The Moon-lit Night

In the huge bowl of the night,
The moon and the stars
Are like egg yolks
Floating in the nightly soup,
Shining.

春天

春天是個魔術師
他用奇妙的功夫
把冰雪溶化
使大地長草
樹木生芽
花卉開花

台灣時報76、7月

Spring

Spring is a magician.
He waves a wonderful wand
To melt ice and snow
and let grass grow,
Trees sprout and
Flowers bloom.

—Taiwan Times, July 1987.

夏天

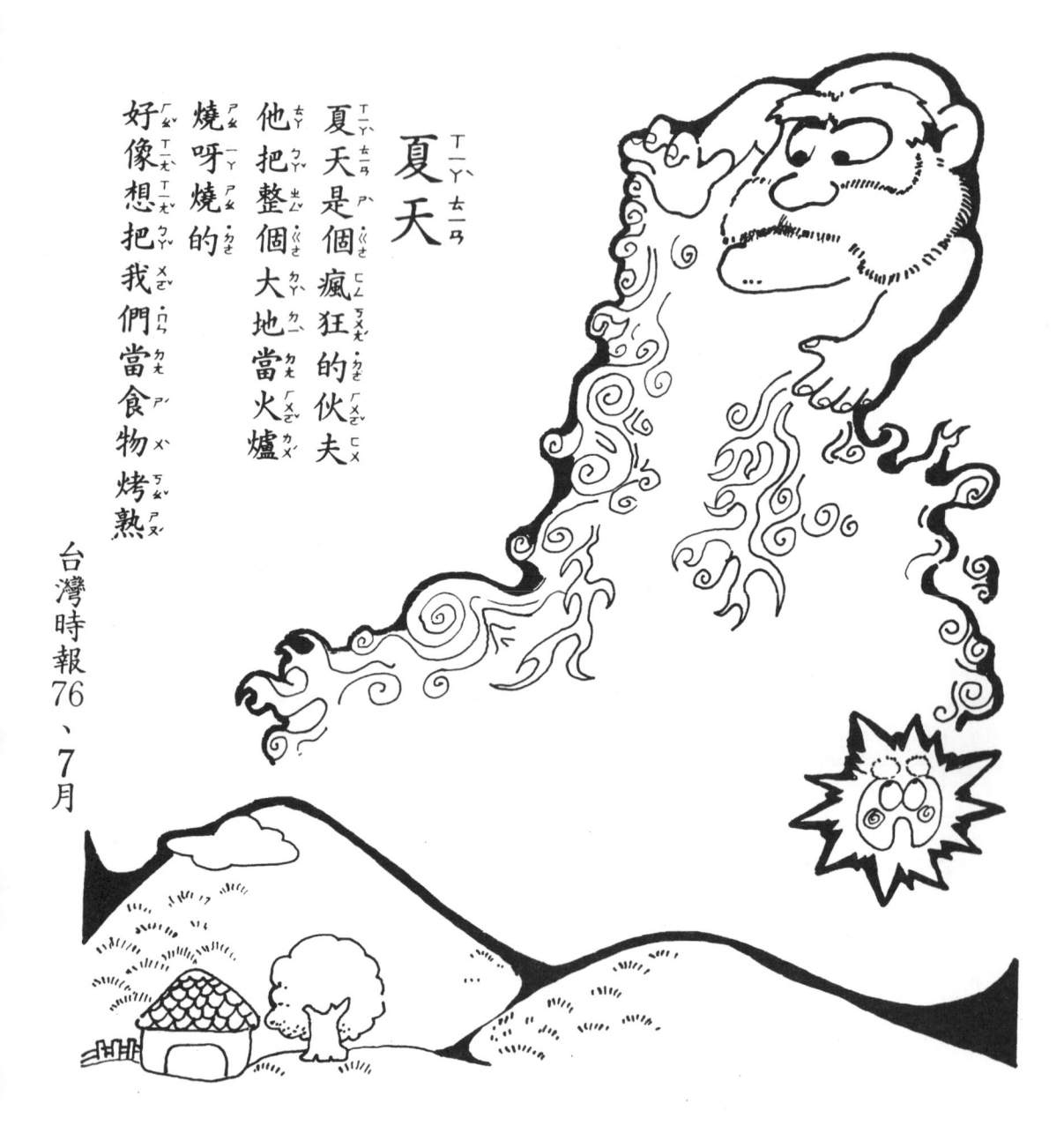

夏天是個瘋狂的伙夫
他把整個大地當火爐
燒呀燒的
好像想把我們當食物烤熟

台灣時報76、7月

Summer

Summer is a crazy cook,
Trying to make the earth a furnace.
Burning and burning, he
Seems to grill us over the fire as food

—Taiwan Times, July 1987.

秋天

秋天是個頑童
他把黃葉亂丟
弄得遍地髒亂
該打屁股

台灣時報76、7月

Autumn

Autumn is a playful boy.
He messes the yellow leaves in a disorderly manner.
He turns everything upside down.
He is naughty and should be disciplined.

—Taiwan Times, July 1987.

冬天

冬天是個神奇的畫家
他一夜之間
就把整個大地畫得清新雪白

台灣時報76、7月

Winter

Winter is an extraordinary painter.
Over a night,
He turns the whole earth into a fresh, snowy world.

—Taiwan Times, July 1987.

春風

沙白

春風是涼爽的天使
她以無形的巨大電扇
吹涼我們
吹涼大地
像默默行善的無名氏
不給人知

66

Spring Breezes

Spring breezes are an angel.
She uses a huge invisible electric fan
To cool us down and
To cool the earth down.
She is silently doing good as an anonymous
    altruist,
Unknown to others.

風箏

沙白

我把我快樂的心掛在風箏上
飄呀!飄的
我要飄到白雲上
駕駛白雲在天上飛來飛去

The Kite

I hang my happy heart on the kite.
It floats and floats.
I want it to float to the white clouds, and
Drive them to fly here and there in the sky.

風

沙白

風是涼爽的天使
她以無形的巨大電扇
吹涼我們
吹涼大地
不收電費
她是最慷慨的人

Wind

Wind is an angel of coolness.
She uses a huge, invisible electric fan
To cool us down and
To cool the earth down
Without charge.
She is the most generous person.

風鈴　沙白

大風吹
小風吹
風鈴大跳大響
風鈴輕搖細響
原來風鈴是風神最乖的女兒
風神教她唱歌跳舞給我們欣賞

國語日報77、3、29

Wind Chimes

A strong gale blows, and
The wind chimes jump noisily and clang loudly.
A breeze blows, and
The wind chimes ring softly.
The wind chimes are the most obedient daughter of
    Wind the Spirit,
Who has taught her to sing and dance for us to enjoy.

    —Guoyu Daily, March 19, 1988.

春遊

沙白

鳥兒和綠葉饗宴綠色大餐
蝴蝶和鮮花饗宴美麗大餐
大地饗宴春陽的溫柔大餐
大家享用自己的豐盛野餐

滿天星76、9

Spring Outing

Birds among green leaves are a feast of greenness.
Butterflies among flowers are a feast of beauty.
The earth in the spring sun is a feast of softness.
Here, we are enjoying our picnic prepared by ourselves.

    —Mantian Xing, September 9, 1987.

山　　沙白

每個山頂都是尖尖的
他們站得那麼高
好像要到天上
摘星星給我們玩

The Mountains

Almost all mountains have pointy tops.
They stand high up,
As if they would reach the sky
To pick the stars for us to play.

雲

白雲像棉花糖
飄在天上
玩來玩去
不久就被太陽吃得光光

The White Clouds

The white clouds are like cotton candies
Floating in the sky.
There they play and play.
Before long they are eaten by the sun.

雨

雨是個愛哭的孩子
自己哭得滿身濕濕的
還要淋濕別人
太陽公公出來後
她就不敢哭了

Rain

Rain is a crybaby.
He soaks himself crying and
Also gets others wet.
As soon as Grandpa Sun appears,
He would stop crying.

—Kindergartens' Magazine, March 1988.

海

她的肚子那麼大
有鯨魚、鮪魚……在游泳
有輪船在行駛
那起伏的波浪
像她的巨大肚皮
搖來搖去
跳着浪花舞

The Sea

How big a belly she has!
There, whales and tuna fish are swimming.
There, ships are sailing.
Waves go up and down.
Like her big belly,
They are swinging and swinging.
They seem to be dancing a wave dance.

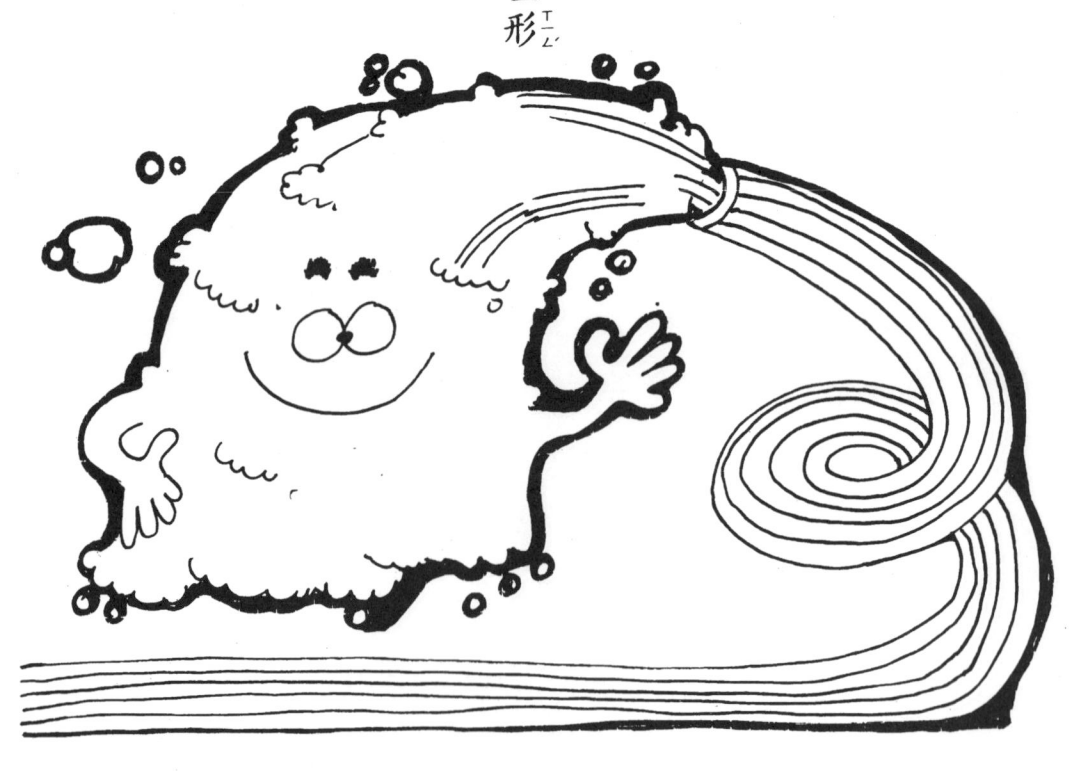

水

水是多變的魔術師，
放在杯裏，變成杯形
放在壺蘆裡，變成壺蘆形
在海裡變成海水
在河裡變成河水
而在我的手裡
就變成好玩的水

Water

Water is a changeable magician.
Put in a cup, it becomes a shape of a cup, and
Put in a pot, a shape of a pot.
In the sea, it becomes sea water, and
In the river, river water.
In my hand, it becomes something fun.

—Taiwan Newspaper, November 15, 1987.

湖　　沙白

湖像一隻大眼睛
仰視奇妙的天空
而更奇妙的天空
是湖底綺麗的幻影

The Lake

The lake is like a huge eye.
Watching the wonderful sky.
Something even more wonderful is
That the sky becomes a beautiful phantom in the lake.

—Taiwan Times, November 22, 1987.

海浪

白沙

海浪是個說謊者
他急速地擁抱了海灘一下
說要跟她結婚
卻急速地逃走了

海浪是個多情人
吻了海灘一次
又吻一次,又一次……
他是世界上最喜歡接吻的人

秋水76、8

A Sea Wave

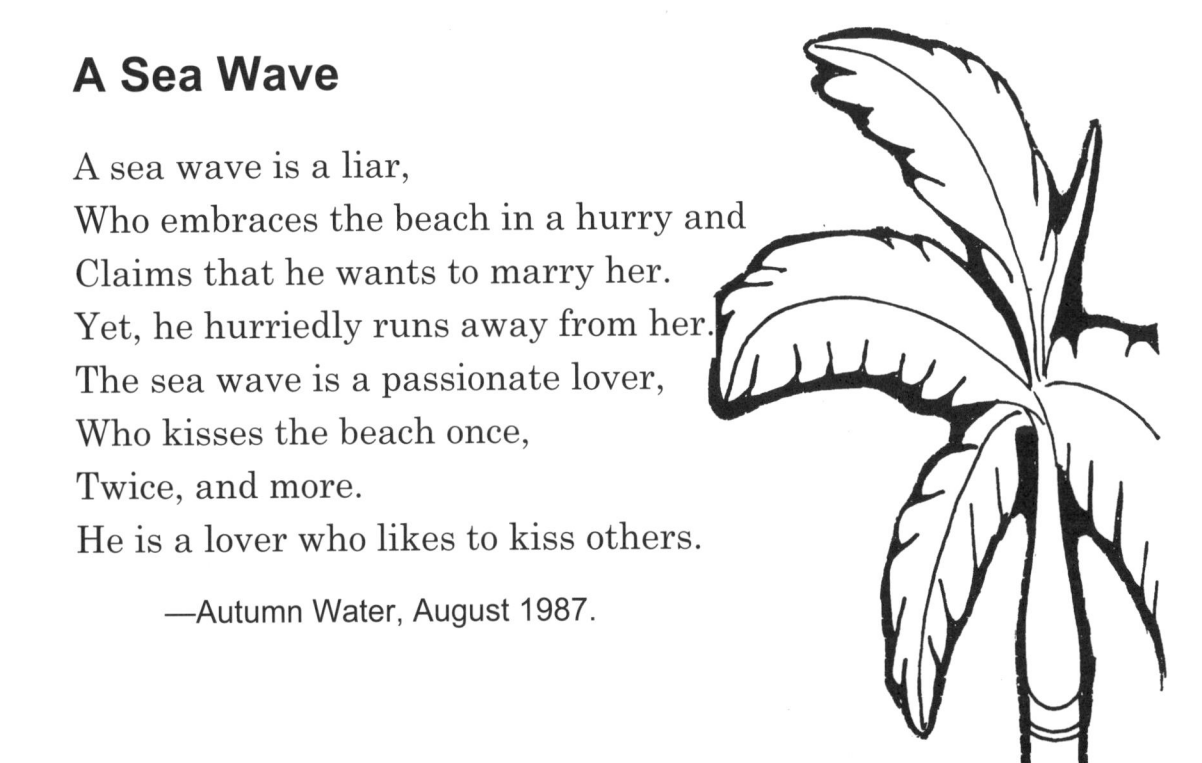

A sea wave is a liar,
Who embraces the beach in a hurry and
Claims that he wants to marry her.
Yet, he hurriedly runs away from her.
The sea wave is a passionate lover,
Who kisses the beach once,
Twice, and more.
He is a lover who likes to kiss others.

—Autumn Water, August 1987.

湍流

沙白

考試時
就像游泳於湍流中
要先有平時訓練的良好技術
才能得高分

Turbulence

Taking an examination is
Like swimming in turbulence.
You ought to have been trained in good skills
To earn a high score.

河流

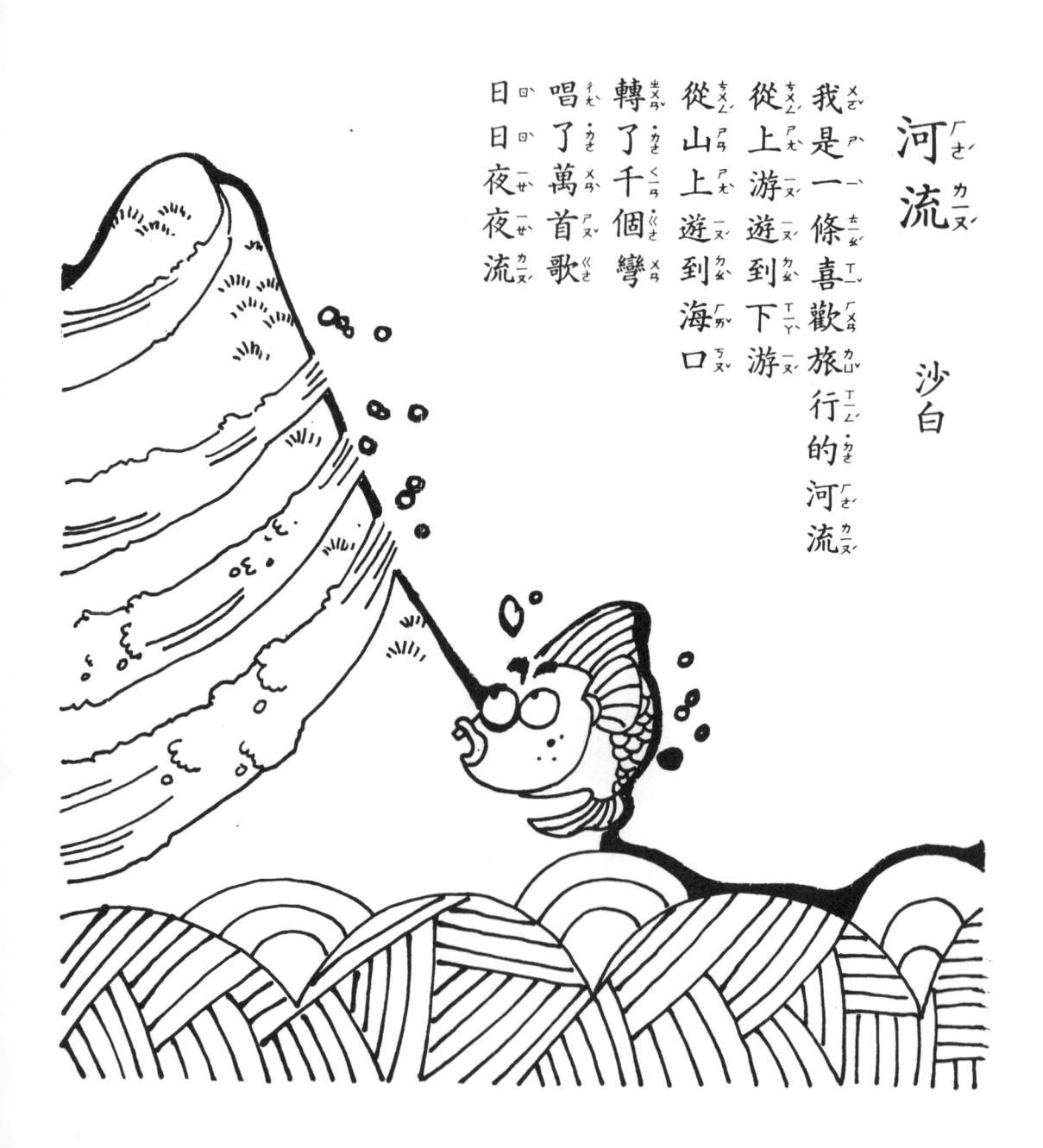

沙白

我是一條喜歡旅行的河流
從上游遊到下游
從山上遊到海口
轉了千個彎
唱了萬首歌
日日夜夜流

A River

I am a river who loves to travel.
I swim from upstream to downstream,
From the mountains to the sea.
I have experienced hundreds upon hundreds
    of curves and
Sung thousands upon thousands of songs.
I flow day and night.

自來水

地球被鑽破後
自來水就汩汩流
流自地球的身體
像人的身體割破流血
地球的身體那麼大
一直流不死
而人的身體那麼小
血流多了就會死
要好好地珍惜

Tap Water

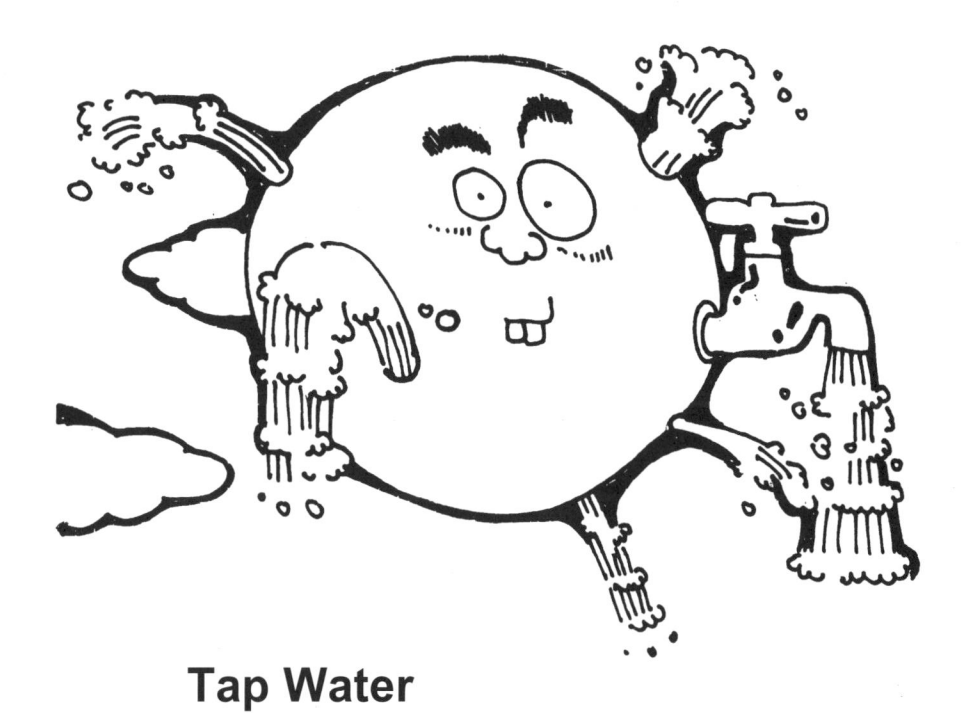

After having been drilled a hole in the earth,
Tap water flows.
Tap water flows from the insides of the earth.
It is like our body which has been cut and
    from which blood flows.
The earth is so huge that
It will not die from the flowing of water.
Yet, my body is small.
If blood keeps flowing from it, I shall die.
We should cherish our body and our earth.

鼻子會唱歌

小弟弟說:「我的鼻子會唱歌。」

媽媽說:「你唱的是感冒鼻塞歌。」

小弟弟問:「為什麼我的鼻子會唱歌?」

媽媽說:「你冬天穿得單薄,玩水玩得太多。以後再這樣子,竹鞭也會咻咻唱歌。」

小弟弟說:「我不敢再這樣子了。」

國語日報76、3、4

The Nose that Can Sing a Song

My little brother says, "My nose can sing a song."
My mother responds, "Your song is about your having caught
    a cold and your having a stuffy nose."
My little brother asks, "Why can my nose sing a song?"
My mother answers, "Your clothes are not enough to guard
    against wintry temperature.
    You have played with water much.
    If you keep doing this,
    whips in my hand would be singing, too."
My little brother says,
    "I wouldn't dare to do these things again."

—Guoyu Newspaper, March 4, 1987.

時間

沙白

時間在我們的眼前飛來飛去,
時間在我們的車外跑來跑去,
像天上的飛雲,
要如何捉住?
飛去的是昨日,
要來的是明日,
而今日,
就像我們釣到的魚,
要好好地抓住,
好好地珍惜,
好好地料理。

Time

Time flies before our eyes.
Time also flies outside our cars,
Like clouds in the sky.
How could we hold it?
That which flew away was yesterday, and
That which is coming is tomorrow.
Today
Is like a fish in our hands.
We have to hold it tightly and
Cherish it and
Cook it well.

鐘

噹！噹！噹
教堂有個鐘
教我們要信神

噹！噹！噹
學校有個鐘
教我們要好好讀書

噹！噹！噹
我們心裡也有一個鐘
教我們要做好人

沙白

The Clock

Ding, dong!
There is a clock on the steeple of the church,
Teaching us to believe in God.

Ding, dong!
There is a clock in the school,
Teaching us to study well.

Ding, dong!
There is also a clock in our heart,
Teaching us to be good.

鐘錶

沙白

好鐘錶是最忠實的時間切割機
他將半天割成十二小時
一小時割成六十分
一分割成六十秒
不慌不忙
絕不投機取巧

The Watch

A good watch is a faithful cutting machine.
He cuts a half day into twelve hours,
An hour into sixty minutes and
A minute into sixty seconds.
He is doing his job leisurely and not in a hurry.
He is not opportunistic in his career as a cutting machine.

手指

沙白

一隻手有五個兄弟
共同合作
從不分離

兩隻手有十個兄弟
大家合作
所向無敵

The Fingers

A hand has five fingers; they are like brothers.
As brothers, they should work cooperatively.
They will not separate.
Two hands have ten fingers.
Working together,
They are invincible.

溫度計

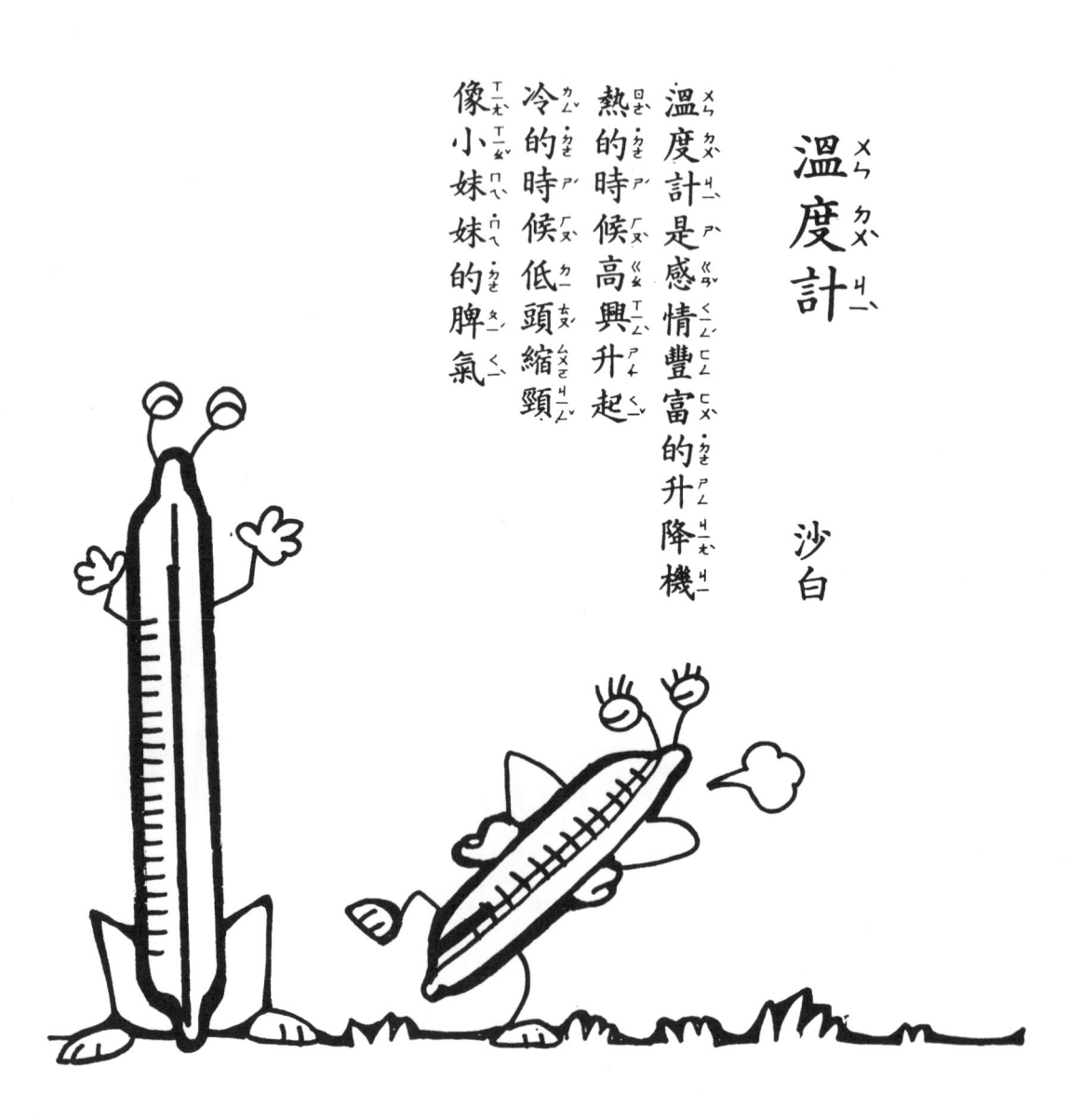

沙白

溫度計是感情豐富的升降機
熱的時候高興升起
冷的時候低頭縮頸
像小妹妹的脾氣

The Barometer

The barometer is like an emotional elevator.
That is, when it is hot, it will rise;
When it is cold, it will shrink and come down
Like the temperament of my little sister.

尺

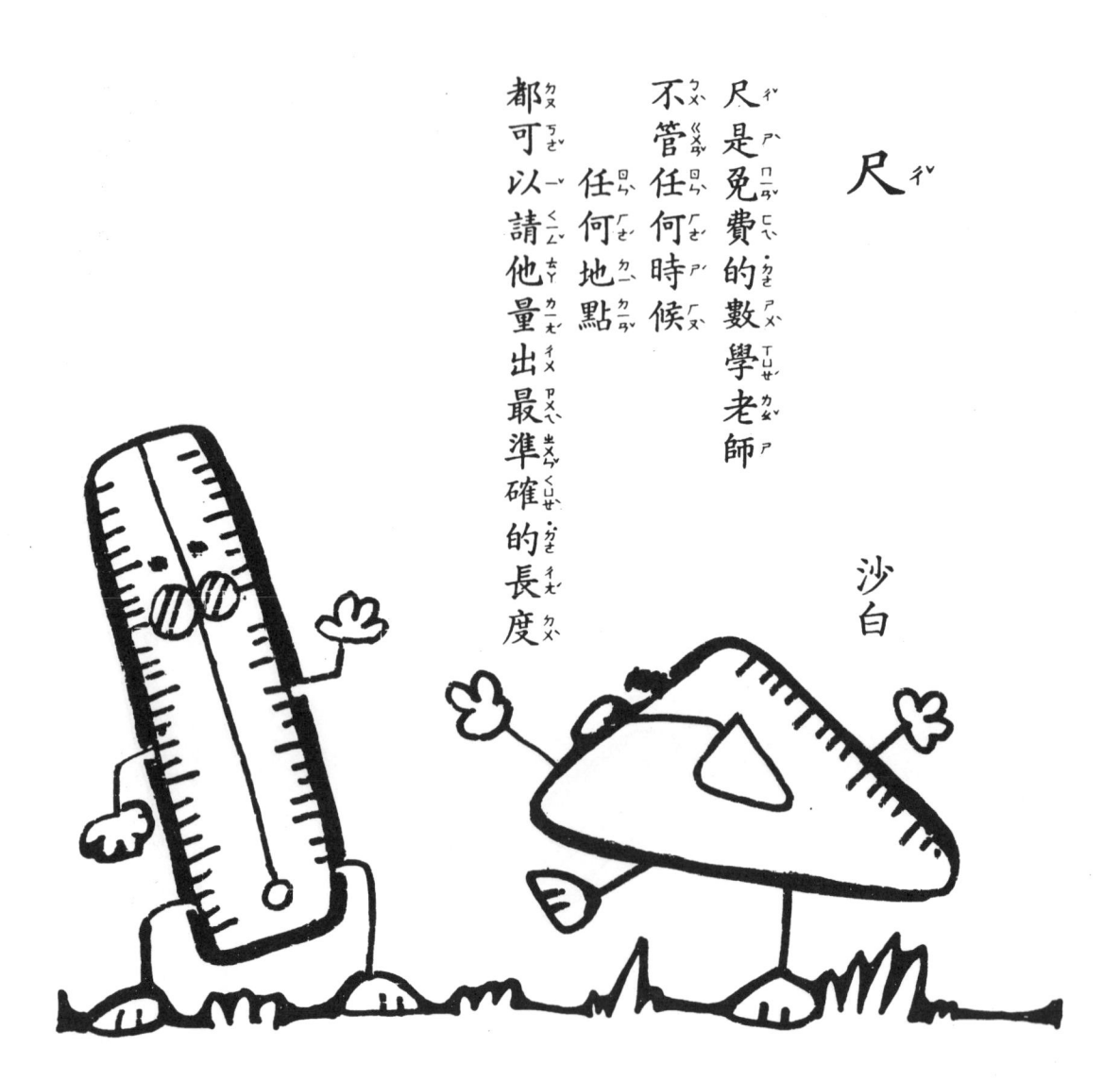

尺是免費的數學老師
不管任何時候
任何地點
都可以請他量出最準確的長度

沙白

The Ruler

The ruler is like a math teacher free of charge.
Any time and
Anywhere,
He will give us exact lengths.

鞋子

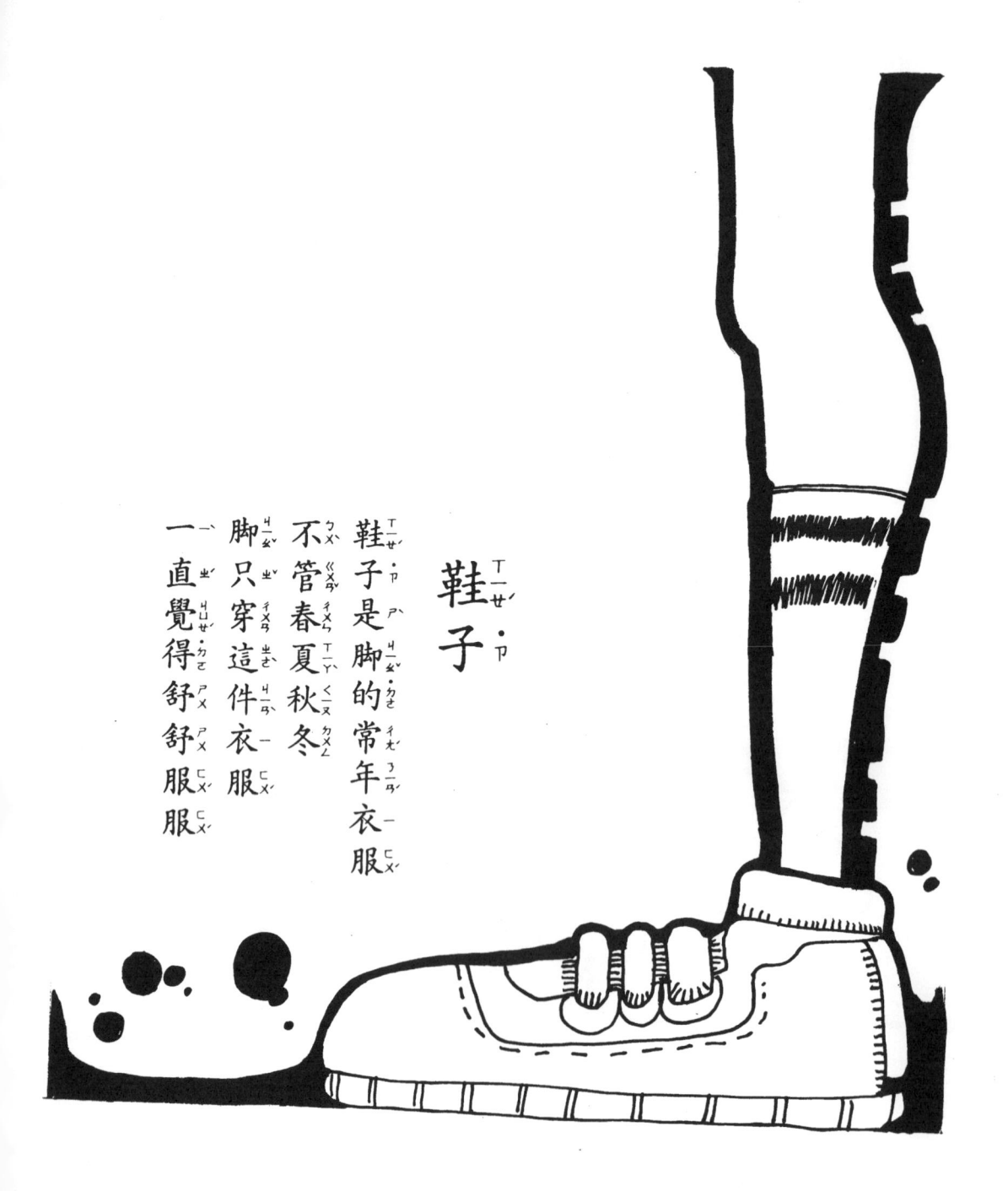

鞋子是脚的常年衣服
不管春夏秋冬
脚只穿這件衣服
一直覺得舒舒服服

Shoes

Shoes are the clothing our feet wear all year around,
In spring, summer, autumn and winter.
Only when the feet wear this clothing,
Would they feel comfortable.

—Taiwan Xinsheng Newspaper, December 13, 1987.

路

路是最堅忍的朋友
天天讓人踏過
車輛走過
卻不會生氣

台灣時報 76·6·28

The Road

The road is the most persevering friend.
People tread on it every day, and
Cars run on it all the time.
He never gets angry.

—Taiwan Times, June 28, 1987.

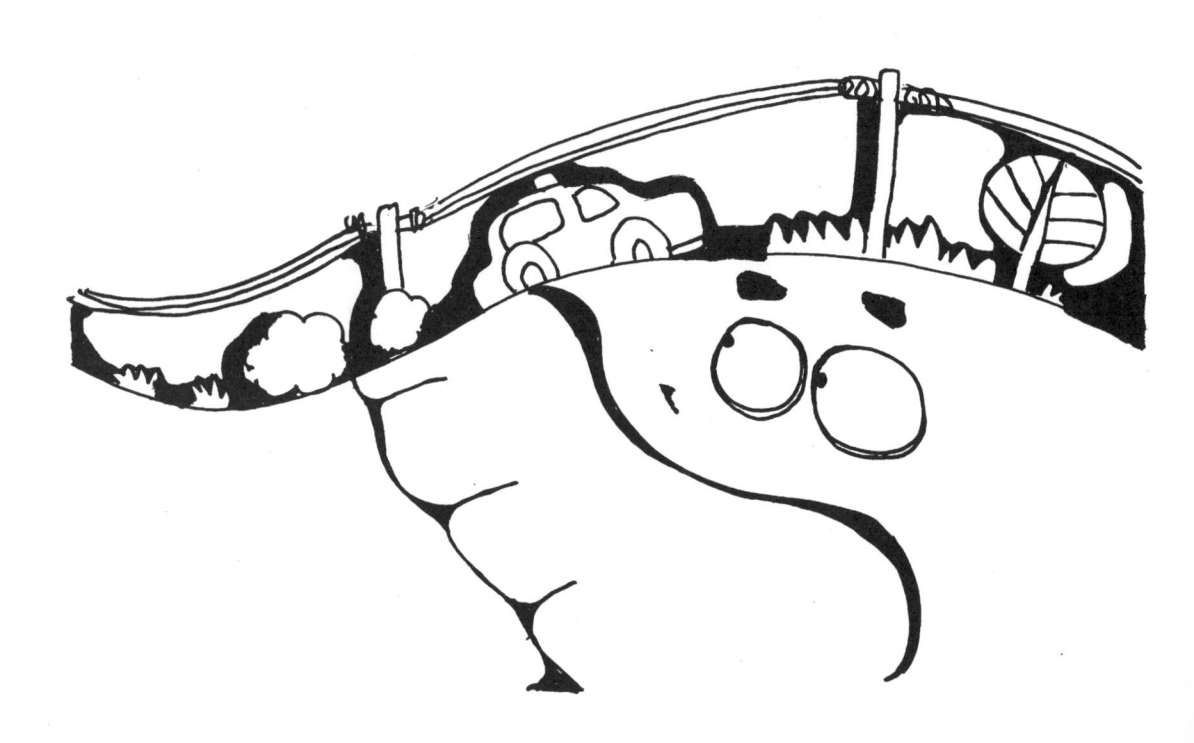

口香糖

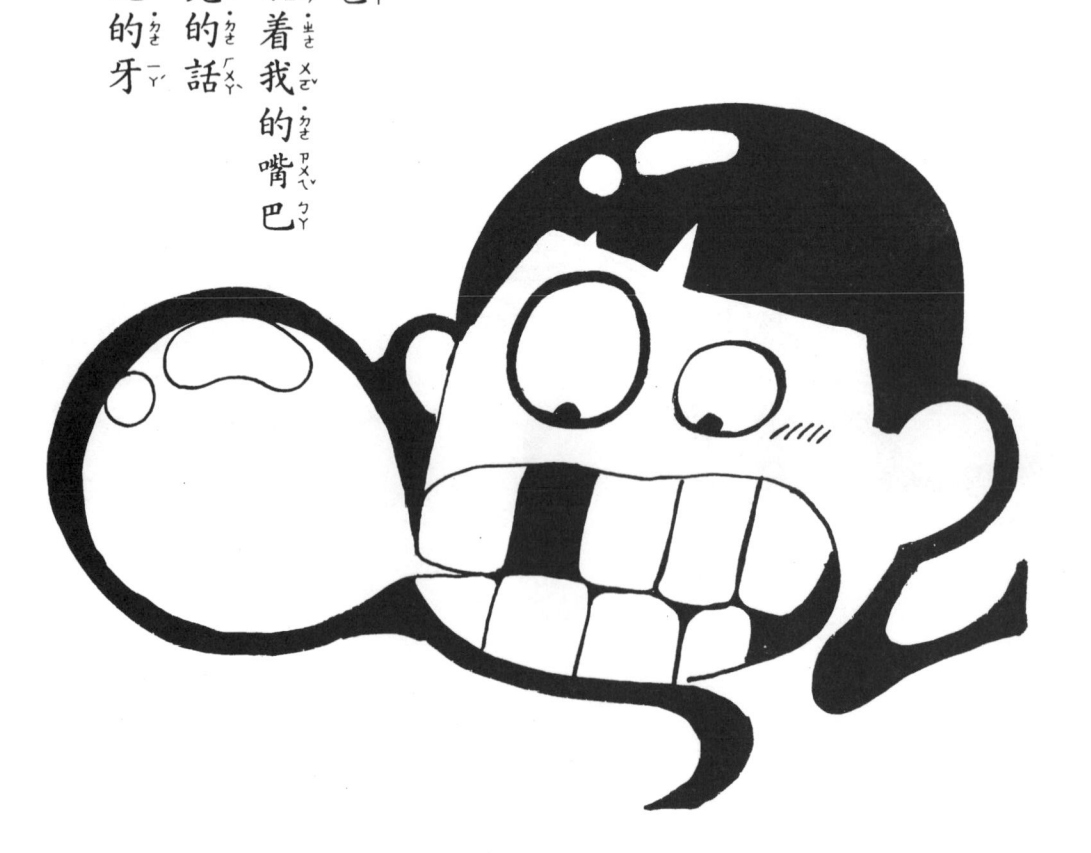

媽媽黏着爸爸
好像口香糖黏着我的嘴巴
媽媽有說不完的話
我也有蛀不完的牙

Chewing Gum

My mother sticks on my father,
Like chewing gum sticking on my mouth.
My mother talks all the time.
I have endless decayed teeth.

茶杯

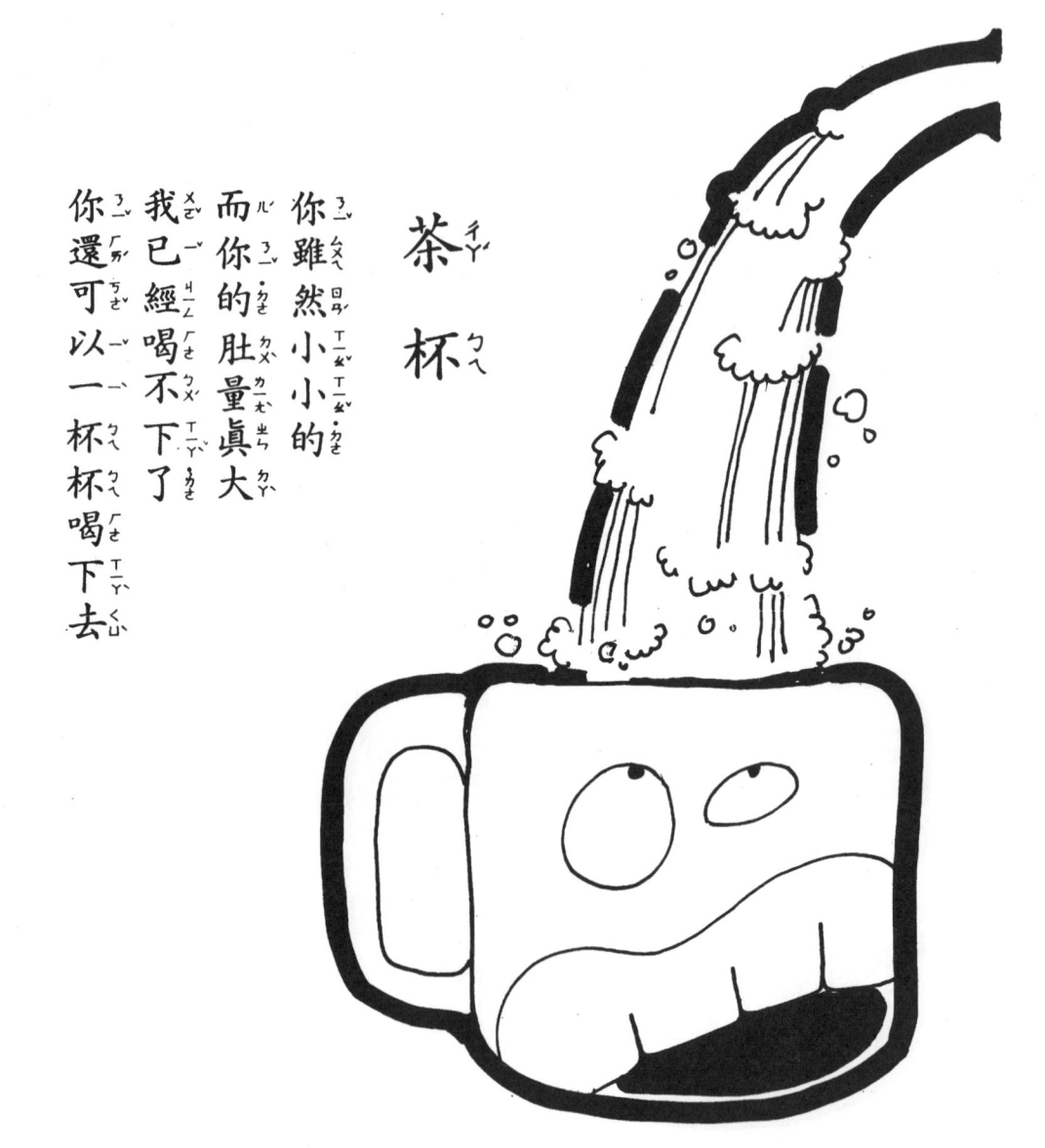

你雖然小小的
而你的肚量真大
我已經喝不下了
你還可以一杯杯喝下去

A Tea Cup

Small as you are;
Yet, you have a big belly.
I have done drinking, but
You still keep being filled all the time.

乞丐

可能是上帝把他們的心腐蝕了吧
可能是上帝把他們的手癱瘓了吧
上帝只賜給他們最可憐的姿態
像滿身生瘡的落水狗
只等待別人的施捨

A Beggar

Perhaps God could have corroded his heart and mind, or
God could have crippled his hands.
God has given him the poorest posture.
He looks like a drowning dog with sores over all the body
Needing others' charity.

衣服

衣服像樹木的花和葉子
一個沒有穿衣服的人
像落葉無花的樹木
難看又可憐
我們要像花開葉茂的樹木
穿着美觀整潔

Clothing

Clothing is like leaves and flowers of a tree.
A naked person is
Like a defoliated tree without leaves and flowers,
Ugly and pitiable.
Like a tree with many leaves and flowers on it,
We should wear clean and beautiful clothes.

公寓人　沙白

每天以坐電梯
實現坐飛機的夢想
而進入小小的公寓後
就像小鳥關在籠裡
失去飛翔的自由

Inhabitants in Apartment Houses

To go home they have to ride elevators
As if their dream of flying in an airplane had come true.
Once they have entered their small apartment houses,
They seem to be locked in bird cages
And lost their freedom of flying.

—Mantian Xing, November 1987.

馬桶

沙白

馬桶的胃口真好
大便小便通通吃掉
假如它有腳
就會爬到廚房
把全部飯菜吃掉

The Toilet Bowl

The toilet bowl has a big appetite,
Swallowing all pee and stool.
If it had feet,
It would crawl to the kitchen and
Eat all the food.

汽車

沙白

像一隻不發脾氣的馬
讓我們坐着
到處旅遊

他是不吃草的鐵馬
讓我們坐着
乾淨又舒服

The Car

Like a tame horse, the car
Carries us
Around for sightseeing.
It is an iron horse without having to eat grass.
It carries us around,
Clean and comfortable.

房屋　沙白

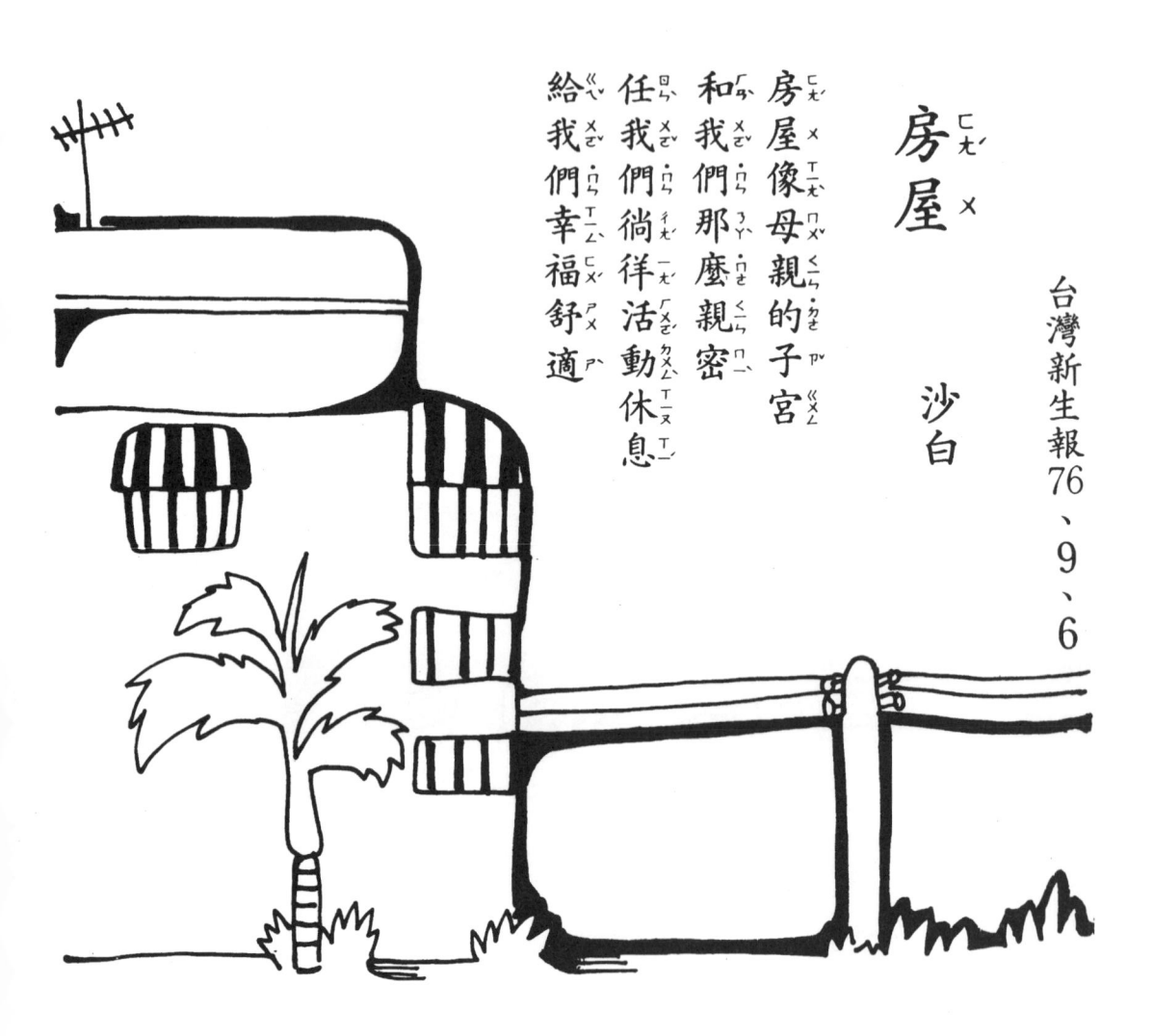

房屋像母親的子宮
和我們那麼親密
任我們倘徉活動休息
給我們幸福舒適

台灣新生報76、9、6

The House

The house is like the mother's womb.
It is intimate with us
Where we take a rest or loiter around and do things.
We feel comfortable in it.

—Taiwan Xinsheng Newspaper, September 6, 1987.

春天

我們有很多春天
雙手抓不完的春天
耳朵聽不完的春天
眼睛看不完的春天

花開鳥叫
使春天熱鬧
而母親的微笑
是最美麗的春天

國語日報76、4、4

Spring

There are so many springs
That we cannot hold them all.
The ear hears endless springs and
The eye sees endless springs.

　　　　　　　　　　Flowers bloom and birds chirp
　　　　　　　　　　Making springs lively.
　　　　　　　　　　It is my mother's smile
　　　　　　　　　　That is the most beautiful spring.

　　　　　　　　　　　　—Guoyu Newspaper, April 4, 1987.

春天

編織美麗的春天
同心協力
所有的花木

春天美妙的歌曲
同聲唱出
所有的鳥兒

跳一跳歡樂的歌舞
也要手牽手
而我們七十億的人類

Spring

All the trees and flowers
Work together
To weave a beautiful spring.

All the birds
Sing in unison
The most wonderful songs of spring.

We the seven billion people on earth
Should, hand in hand,
Sing and dance happily.

樹木

舉起數十支手臂
展開數萬隻綠色手指
向太陽吸食光能營養
在春天裡搔首弄姿

Trees

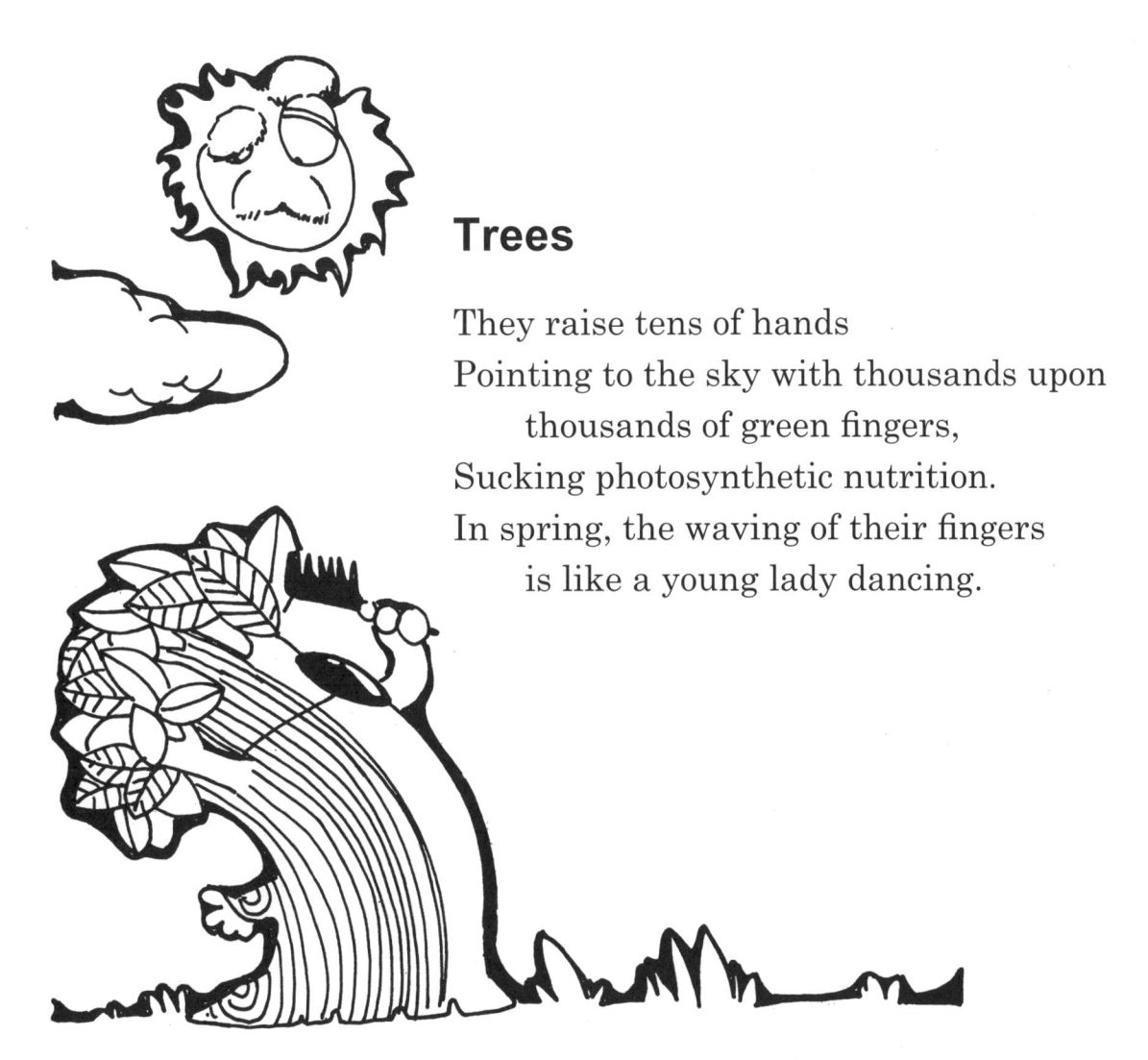

They raise tens of hands
Pointing to the sky with thousands upon
    thousands of green fingers,
Sucking photosynthetic nutrition.
In spring, the waving of their fingers
    is like a young lady dancing.

老榕樹

老榕樹長滿了鬍鬚
結滿了果實
像滿臉長鬚的老公公
帶着一群孫子孫女
在草地上休息

The Old Banyan Tree

The old banyan tree has a lot of beard.
In it, there are a lot of fruit among green leaves.
The tree is like a grandpa with long beard,
Carrying a group of grandchildren
To take a rest on the meadows.

—Taiwan Times, December 12, 1987.

柳樹

在歡樂的春風裡
柳樹像美麗的少女
戴着纖纖碧綠的面紗
照着湖面鏡子
婀娜自喜

The Willow Tree

In the gleeful spring breezes,
The willow tree, like a pretty young lady,
Wears a silky, green veil.
She is looking at herself in the mirror-like lake,
And is enjoying herself gracefully.

—Taiwan Times, December 13, 1987.

樹下讀書

我在樹下讀書,樹也教我讀書。

樹說:

「小朋友,我告訴你,我天天向上生長,就是天天在求進步,邁向更高的理想;我天天向下紮根,就是天天在打深厚的基礎,使自己站得更穩;我的樹葉愈長愈茂盛,我的蔭影就愈大,乘涼的人愈多,我的積德就愈厚。」

Studying under the Tree

I study under the tree.
It seems that the tree is also teaching me how to study hard.
The tree seems to say,
    "My little friend, let me tell you.
      I grow upward every day.
      I make some progress every day
      Desiring to achieve some higher goal.
      Conversely, my roots grow downward,
      Trying to build a solid base every day,
      Which will make me stand on a firmer, deeper footing.
      Then, my leaves would be flourishing.
      As time goes on, there would be more shade
      To shelter more people.
      Thus, I would be beneficial to them and do good to them."

竹(ㄓㄨˊ)

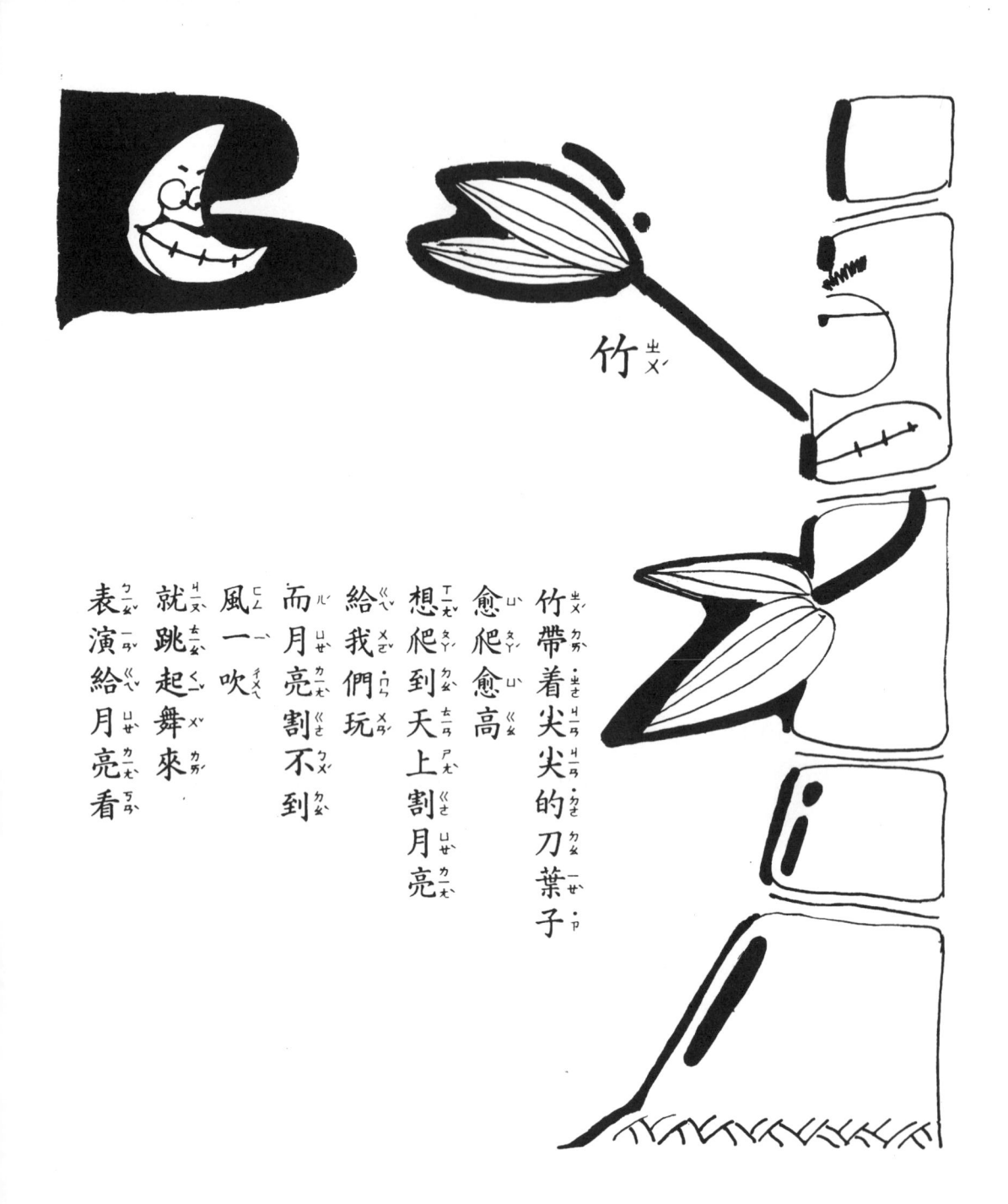

竹帶着尖尖的刀葉子
愈爬愈高
想爬到天上割月亮
給我們玩
而月亮割不到
風一吹
就跳起舞來
表演給月亮看

The Bamboo Tree

The bamboo tree carries its knife-like leaves
To reach high places.
The tree seems to reach the sky and
    cut down the moon
For us to play.
Yet, the tree is unable to do so.
The wind blows and the leaves dance
To play for the moon to enjoy.

紅蘿蔔

你全身通紅
精力充沛
像偉大的關公
大家來多吃
好好學關公

Carrot

You are red all over your body,
Full of energy,
Like General Guangong the Great.
Let us eat more of carrot and
Be like Guangong.

螢火蟲　沙白

螢火蟲向貧窮的學生說：

「書上有光、有能、有知識，

書裡的光比太陽大，

書裡的能比原子能強，

書裡的知識比孔子、耶穌和釋迦多，

用我的光，就能夠照耀所有的知識寶庫。」

The Firefly

The firefly says to a poor student,
"There are light, power, and knowledge in the book.
There the light is brighter than that of the sun.
The power is stronger than that of atomic energy.
The knowledge is more than that of Confucius,
Jesus Christ, and the Buddha.
If you make good use of my light,
It is possible for you to use it to unlock the treasure box
　　of knowledge.

蝴蝶

花開了
蝴蝶一群群飛來
吻花擁花
跳舞給花看

花謝了
蝴蝶就不見了
原來蝴蝶是採花賊

沙白

The Butterflies

Flowers bloom and
Invite a lot of butterflies.
The butterflies kiss the flowers
And dance for them to enjoy.

The flowers fade, and
The butterflies vanish.
They are flower-picking thieves.

啄木鳥

沙白

啄木鳥想當外科醫師
牠將樹木開刀後
只顧啄蟲自己吃
却忘了縫合傷口
所以牠不是人類的醫師
而是樹木的醫師

Woodpeckers

Woodpeckers want to be surgeons.
They operate on trees and
Pick worms out for themselves to eat.
They forget to stitch the openings.
They are not surgeons of us humans.
They are doctors of the trees.

牛

一隻牛十人工
十隻牛百人工
拖了牛車
還要到田裡做工
不吃飯不吃肉
不吃糖不吃魚
只吃沒人要的草
卻力大無比
吃苦耐勞

The Ox

One ox can do work as ten people.
Ten oxen can do work as a hundred people.
An ox should pull a cart,
And then work in the fields.
It eats only grass
Without having to eat rice, meat,
Sugar, or fish.
It has immense power and
Is able to endure hardships.

動物園

沙白

動物園是動物的國際都市
有許多國的動物移民——
美國的野牛、非洲的犀牛
台灣山貓、北極熊、企鵝
各國動物都住在這裡
像東京、紐約和巴黎
有各國的移民
真是多彩多姿

A Zoo

A zoo is animals' international city.
There are animal immigrants from
    many countries—
American buffalos, African rhinos,
Taiwan lynxes, North Pole bears,
    and Penguins from the South Pole.
Animals from many countries live here.
The zoo is like a big city like Tokyo,
    New York or Paris,
Where immigrants from other countries live.
The zoo is truly colorful and wonderful.

烏龜

沙白

在陸上
你拖着戰車走
在水裡
你揹着戰車游
你是個兩棲陸戰隊戰士
請你載我去水裡抓魚
請你載我到原野遊戲

The Tortoise

On land,
You walk pulling a tank.
In the water,
You swim bearing a tank.
You are an amphibious marine corps warrior.
Please carry me to catch fish in the water, and
Please take me to play in the wild fields.

作者 簡介

■ 沙白，本名涂秀田，一九四四年生，台灣省屏東縣人。屏東初中，台北建國高中畢業，高雄醫學院畢業，日本國立東京大學研究。

■ 沙白自幼年即習中國古典文學，青少年時，更吸取西洋文學和日本文學等，而成為融合中西文學思想的詩人。

■ 曾任現代詩頁月刊主編，阿米巴詩社社長，南杏社長，笠詩社社務委員，心臟詩社社長、布穀鳥詩社同仁，高雄市文藝夏令營講師，亞洲詩人大會和世界詩人大會籌備委員。

■ 曾應邀參加一九八六年漢城亞洲詩人大會，一九八八年台中亞洲詩人大會，和一九八八年第十屆曼谷世界詩人大會發表論文〈詩是現代社會最重要的空氣〉，獲大會極高評價，曼谷英文大報THE NATION（國民報）以首頁引介此文。一九九〇年長沙世界華文兒童文學會議，艾青作品國際學術研討會。

■ 曾獲中華民國新詩學會詩運獎、朗誦詩獎、高雄市文藝獎、中華民國兒童文學會獎入圍（第二名獎）、心臟詩獎、柔蘭獎、亞洲詩人大會感謝狀、高雄市牙醫師公會和中華民國牙醫師公會感謝獎、台灣文學家牛津獎候選人。

■ 現任臺一社發行人，《大海洋》詩社社長、中國文藝協會會員、中華民國新詩學會候補監事、世界詩人會會員、世界華人詩人協創會理事、中華民

- 國兒童文學會會員、台灣省兒童文學會會員、高雄市兒童文學寫作學會理事長、六堆雜誌編委、中華民國牙醫師公會編委。
- 著作：詩集『河品』、詩集『太陽的流聲』（中華民國兒童文學獎入圍）、中英文詩集『空洞的貝殼』（余光中、陳靖奇譯）、童詩集『星星亮晶晶』、『星星愛童詩』、童詩集『唱歌的河流』（中華民國兒童文學獎入圍）、『沙白散文集』、『沙白詩文集』、傳記『不死鳥田中角榮』、『毛澤東隱蹤之謎（補著）』、『牙科知識』、『快樂的牙齒』等，以及T.S艾略特和保羅、梵樂希等英日文學之翻譯和介紹。作品曾被翻譯為英、日、韓文等，在外國及中國大陸曾介紹過。
- 留美：哈佛大學、波士頓大學植牙中心。
- 中華民國口腔植體醫學會專科醫師、台灣牙醫植體醫學會專科醫師、國際口腔植牙專科醫師學會院士、前中華民國口腔植體醫學會監事及專科醫師甄審委員、美國矯正學會會員。
- 國際詩人獎、榮譽文學博士、ABI及IBC國際傑出名人獎、美國文化協會國際和平獎；曾獲兩次國際植牙會議論文第二名獎。
- 沙白詩作列入韓國慈山李相斐博士出版的「現代世界代表詩人選集」。
- 現職：台立牙科診所院長
- 住址：高雄市新興區仁愛一街二二八號
        高雄市前金區中華三路一三五路
- 電話：（〇七）二三六七六〇二
- 手機：〇九一九一八〇八七五
- e-mail：shiutientu@gmail.com
- e-mail：taiyi.implant@msa.hinet.net
- 網址：www.taili-dentist.com.tw
- 郵政劃撥：04596534涂秀田帳戶

An Introduction to Tu Shiu-tien (Sar Po)

Born on July 28, 1944 at Toulun Village, Zhutian Township, Pingdong County, Taiwan Province, Republic ofChina.

Education:

Zhutian Primary School, Pingdong;
Provincial Pingdong Middle School;
Jianguo High School, Taipei;
Department of Dentistry, Kaohsiung Medical College.

Foreign institutions where he pursued further studies and research:

Research Institute of Dentistry, National University of Tokyo;
Osaka University of Dentistry;
National University of Osaka;
Research Institute of Dentistry, Harvard University;
Center for Dental Implantation, Boston University.

Interests :

Chinese classics, Western literature, Japanese literature. Oriental and Occidental philosophy and Thoughts on the Arts and their theory.

Honors and Awards :

Award for Writing of Poetry, Kaohsiung.
Award for Chanting of Poetry, Kaohsiung.
Award for the Arts and Literature, Kaohsiung.
Roelan Award, Kaohsiung.
Award from the Society of Cardiology.
Award from the Republic of China Association of New Poetry.
Outstanding prizes from International Poets' Association, ABI (American Biographical Institute) and IBC (International Biographical Center).
Award from the International Society of Poets

A certificate of an academician in the Association of International Dental Implantation Specialists at the University of New York.
Honorary Degree of Doctor of Literature (Litt. D.)
Outstanding People of the 20th-century American Biographical Institute (ABI) and the International Biographical Center (IBC)
Award from the American Cultural Agency for Promotion of World Peace.
Second Award in the presentation of a paper at the International Congress of Oral Implantologists (ICOI), twice.
2004 International Peace Prize, for outstanding achievement to the good of society as a whole, by the authority of the United Cultural Convention sitting in the United States of America.
2005 as one of the Top 100 Writers in Poetry and Literature, witnessed by the Officers of the International Biographical Center at its Headquarters in Cambridge, England.
2005 Lifetime of Achievement One Hundred, signed at the Headquarter of the International Biographical Center of Cambridge, England.

Current Occupation :

Dentist, Taiyi Dental Clinic and Taiyi Dental Implantation Center.

Associations :

President, the Amoeba Poetical Association, Kaohsiung Medical College.
Editor-in-Chief, the Modern Poetry Monthly,
President, the Nanxing Magazine,
President, the Big Ocean Association of Poetry;
A committee member for general affairs, the Li Journal of Poetry;
A lecturer, Kaohsiung Summer Camp;
Associate convener, the section of poetry, Kaohsiung Qingxi Association of the Arts;
Supervisor, the Southern Branch, the Chinese Association of the Arts and Literature;
An editor, the Liudui Magazine;
A preparatory Committee Member, the Asian Poet Conference;
A committee member, the World Olympic Association of Poetry;
An academician, College of World Culture;
Honorary Doctor, World Conference of the Poets.

Classification of His Works:

Collections of Poetry:

Hepin (So. The Streams), Preface by Zhu Chendong, "The Realm of Poetry—a Discussion of Sar Po's Poetry." Taipei: Modern Poetry Club, March 1966.

The Spiritual Sea. Kaohsiung: Taiyi She, September 1990.

The Hollow Shells, with Chinese and English texts, tr. by Yu Guangzhong and Ching-chi Chen. Kaohsiung: Taiyi She, December 1990.

The Streaming Voices of the Sun, in the Collection of Taiwanese Poets, #18, ed. the Li Journal of Poetry. Kaohsiung: Chunhui Publishing Co., November 2019.

Essays on His Poetics:

Sar Po's Essays on His Poetics. Kaohsiung: Chunhui Publishing Co., August 2020.

Prose:

Sar Po's Essays. Taipei: Linbai Publishing Co., September 1988.

Children's Literature:

「星星亮晶晶」Twinkle, Twinkle, Little Stars. Kaohsiung: Taiyi She, October 1986.
「星星愛童詩」Stars Love Children's Poetry. Kaohsiung: Taiyi She, September 1987.
「唱歌的河流」Singing Rivers. Kaohsiung: Taiyi She, September 1990.

Biography :

An Undying Bird, Tanaka Kakuei (不死鳥田中角榮). (In serialization, Taiwan Times.) Tainan: Xibei Publishing Co., May 1984.

Books on Dental Hygiene :

Knowledge on Dentistry. Kaohsiung: Taiyi She, August 1987.
The Happy Teeth. Taizhong: The Commission of Education, Taiwan Provincial Government, April 1993.

Translation of Texts and Theories of literature, Taiwan and Overseas:

"T.S. Eliot, 'The Dirty Salvages'", from English into Chinese, in Sar Po's Essays on His Poetics, pp. 256-273.
"Paul Valery's Literary Theory, One." in Sar Po's Essays on His Poetics, pp. 280-285.
"Paul Valery's Literary Theory, Two." in Sar Po's Essays on His Poetics, pp. 286-294.
"Paul Valery's Literary Theory, Three." in Sar Po's Essays on His Poetics, pp. 295-299.
"Paul Valery's Literary Theory, Four." in Sar Po's Essays on His Poetics, pp. 300-307.
"Paul Valery's Literary Theory, Five." in Sar Po's Essays on His Poetics, pp. 308-312.
"Paul Valery's Literary Theory, Six." in Sar Po's Essays on His Poetics, pp. 313-317.
"Paul Valery's Literary Theory, Seven." in Sar Po's Essays on His Poetics, pp. 318-325.
"On Something about Charles Baudelaire" by Kuritsu Norio, in Sar Po's Essays on His Poetics, pp. 326-336.

"On Charles Baudelaire" by Kuritsu Norio, in Sar Po's Essays on His Poetics, pp. 337-350-349.
"On Charles Baudelaire and His Poetical Language" by Kuritsu Norio, in Sar Po's Essays on His Poetics, pp.350-360.
"On Charles Baudelaire and His Prose" by Kuritsu Norio, in Sar Po's Essays on His Poetics, pp. 361-370.
"On the Pains of Charles Baudelaire" by Kuritsu Norio, in Sar Po's Essays on His Poetics, pp. 371-374.
"On Rambo" by Kuritsu Norio, in Sar Po's Essays on His Poetics, pp. 375-382.
"A Dream Inside and Out, Two Poems," by Shinkawa Kasue, in Sar Po's Essays on His Poetics, pp. 432-433.
"Two Poems by Yamamura Bocho," in Sar Po's Essays on His Poetics, pp. 436-437.
"Some Ideas on Taiwan Poets" by Kaneko Hideo, in Sar Po's Essays on His Poetics, pp. 438-439.
"Kawada Kakuei, Mushanokoji Saneatsu, Chen Tingshi," in Sar Po's Essays on His Poetics.
Papers Read in Conferences:

Papers read at the International Conference for Dental Implantation; Presented twice and awarded twice.
"Poetry Is the Most Important Air in Our Modern Society," read at the World Poets' Congress, Bangkok, Thailand, 1988; the speech was published in *The Nation*, Bangkok, Tailand.

譯者 簡介

◙ **陳靖奇**
◙ 出生：台灣省雲林縣古坑鄉。
◙ 幼兒園：雲林縣斗六糖廠附設幼兒園。
◙ 國小：雲林縣古坑國民小學。
　　　　台北市西門國民小學。
◙ 初中：台北建國中學。
◙ 高中：台北成功中學。
◙ 學士：國立臺灣師範大學英語學系。
◙ 碩士：國立臺灣師範大學英語研究所。
◙ 博士：美國明尼蘇達大學美國研究所。
　重點研究：美國文學與文化，「二十世紀三零時代的美國左翼文學，
　普羅大眾與資本社會的矛盾等議題。」

◙ 經歷：
　台北市立景美女子高級中學英語科教師。
　私立大同工學院講師。
　國立高雄師範大學教授兼夜間部主任。
　國立高雄師範大學教授兼英語學系主任。
　國立高雄師範大學教授兼英語研究所所長。
　國立高雄師範大學教授兼文學院院長。
　國立空中大學高雄學習中心主任。
　私立和春技術學院教授兼副校長。
　私立致遠管理學院教授兼應用英語學系主任。

Translated by Prof. Ching-chi Chen, Ph.d.

- Born at Gukeng, Yunlin, Taiwan, Republic of China.

◼ Educated:

- B.A. and M.A., National Taiwan Normal University, majoring in English.

- Ph.D., University of Minnesota, U.S.A., majoring in American studies (social sciences about America and American literature).

◼ Positions held:

- Professor of English, Department of English, National Kaohsiung Normal University.

- Chairperson, the Department of English, National Kaohsiung Normal University.

- Dean, College of the Liberal Arts, National Kaohsiung Normal University.

- Vice President, Hochun Institute of Technology at Daliao, Kaohsiung.

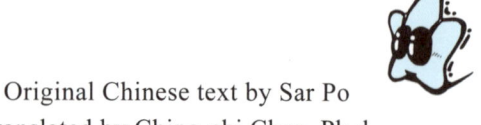

國家圖書館出版品預行編目(CIP)資料

星星愛童詩 = Stars Love Children's Poetry /
沙白著；陳靖奇譯. -- 三版. -- 高雄市：
台一社, 民110.09
　面； 公分
中英對照
ISBN 978-626-95122-1-8 (平裝)

863.598　　　　　　　　110015155

Original Chinese text by Sar Po
Translated by Ching-chi Chen, Ph.d.
Published by Shiu-tien Tu
Chinese and English texts copyright 2021 by Shiu-tien Tu
ALL RIGHTS RESERVED

星星愛童詩
Stars Love Children's Poetry

（榮獲高雄市文藝獎）

著　　者：沙白 Sar Po
翻　　譯：陳靖奇 Ching-chi Chen, Ph.d.
發 行 人：涂秀田
出　　版：台一社
發 行 所：800高雄市新興區仁愛一街228號
電　　話：886-7-2367603; 886-9-19180875
印　　刷：德昌印刷廠股份有限公司
電　　話：886-7-3831238
郵政劃撥：04596534 涂秀田帳戶
登 記 證：行政院新聞局局版業字第4771號
中華民國七十六年九月十五日初版
中華民國七十七年四月十五日二版
中華民國一一〇年九月十五日三版
Email：shiutientu@gmail.com
　　　：taiyi.implant@msa.hinet.net
WWW：TAIYI.egolife.com
　　　：taili-dentist.com.tw

版權所有・翻印必究　　定價新台幣350元(美金15元)